Corridors of Guilt

JOHN BUXTON HILTON

Corridors of Guilt

A Superintendent Kenworthy novel

St. Martin's Press
New York

Library of Congress Cataloging in Publication Data

Hilton, John Buxton.
    Corridors of guilt.

    I. Title.
PR6058.I5C6   1984   823'.914   83-21255
ISBN 0-312-17003-3

First published in Great Britain in 1984 by William Collins Sons
& Co. Ltd.

First U.S. Edition

10 9 8 7 6 5 4 3 2 1

Corridors of Guilt

CHAPTER 1

Yeah. Fuzz both sides all the way up from the station. Then they shoved us up the bleeding back streets, didn't even see a bleeding shop. Pubs all closed, see, blokes moaning on the corners like we was to blame. Then this big bastard, all silver leaves on his cap, four rows of bleeding medal ribbons, he don't like the way we're looking at him, see, so he calls us out the crowd. Yeah. Me and Arfer and Willy, we has to go to his car and we has to turn our pockets out, and when Arfer takes his hand out, he still has four 2p pieces sticking out his knuckles, keeps them there on purpose, see, and this top pig says, 'That's an offensive weapon,' he says. 'I could do you for that.'

Rehearsal. Things to tell Dud and Kevin in Stan's, Monday morning. Living. Experience. A sort of game in which you scored points. Catching the fuzz's eye, getting them worked up, that was one. Being pulled out of the mob, searched for drugs or weapons, two. Three if they took something off you till after the match, like they did Arfer's belt at Romford, so he had to stand an hour and a half holding his trousers up, and Christ, they were only paper-fasteners, not studs.

Five if you won a battle of words.

Come on, son, keep moving. Keep moving, there.

'S a free country, innit?

You had to hand it to Arfer. Had an answer for them every time. Never had to stop and think.

Finsbury v Gorleston, two Saturdays running, one home, one away. Geoff hadn't been to Gorleston before, Christ, what a bleeding dump. He was seventeen, mean eyes wandering without imagination about the crowd, looking for a laugh at the graffiti aerosolled on the tar-washed fences, stocking up with tales for Dud and Kev. His thin limbs jutted from frayed cuffs and turn-ups like an Edwardian warning of the dangers of masturbation. Arfer was two years older, curled his lip cynically at everything they saw. Neither of them had ever been in work, unless you counted Work Experience. Bleeding yard-sweeping experience at twenty-three quid a week. And they had Willy with them. Twelve. A bleeding liability, proud as a prick in his supporter's scarf, making you want to take him one across his north and south. Only the Old Woman paid their fares if they got Willy off her bloody back on a Saturday.

Now they were passing the sooty back gardens of terraced houses. Someone picked up a fist-sized flint, flung it up in a casual parabola. Glass shattered. Somebody's greenhouse. It brought up a cheer from the column. Then they were in the road that led to the ground, the Finsbury battle-cry when they caught sight of the Gorleston bastards, being chivvied along the opposite pavement, pushed in through separate gates, segregated in the stands.

'There's them two from last week.'

Punks. Orange hair, green hair, in stand-up spikes. Got to watch out for them two afterwards. And what a bloody match: goalless draw, for the second week running.

Use your eyes, Ref. Put your bloody specs on.

He don't want specs. What he wants is a bloody guide-dog.

Because he sent Barry Kelly off in the first quarter-hour.

Honest, I'm not kidding, it took eight coppers to get that bloody ref to the changing-room at the end of the first half, dinnit?

After the game, the police cordon parted long enough

for the fringes of the two crowds to overlap. Arfer pushed
Willy in front of him.

'Bloody Finsbury.'

'Bleeding Gorleston.'

An orange head and a green head were trying to turn
between chestnut palings into an alley between houses, a
constable treading on their toes.

'Keep moving. Stay with the crowd.'

'We live up Tanner's Row, see?'

The policeman let them go. Geoff and Arfer followed.
'Tanner's Row.' Willy got pushed away from them.

'Hey! We've lost Willy!'

'He can find his way to the bloody station, can't he?'

'We've got his ticket.'

'He's got a bleeding tongue in his head, ha'n't he?'

The hum of the crowd had become muffled, distant.
The punks took a long time before they turned round.

'You gits following us?'

' 'S a free country, innit?'

Orangehead dived for Geoff's privates. Geoff recoiled,
and the punk's forearm shot under his groin, lifted him
helplessly waist-high. Arfer knew he ought to do
something, but Greenhead had his arms pinioned,
brought the edge of a metal-cored boot down the length
of his shin, stamped his heel on his instep, all his weight
on it. Then he jumped clear, and Arfer fell writhing.
Geoff, his scrotum crushed by Orangescalp's arm, was
screaming to be put down. Orangescalp cast him away
like a rag doll, landing cheek-and-shoulder on the cinder
path.

*Then these two fellers came up, see, and the punks was
away liked greased shit. And I thought, Jesus H. Christ,
it's the bogies. But 'That wasn't all that clever,' one of
them said. 'Before you start mixing it with cowboys like
that, you want to learn suffink. We'd better take you in
hand. 'Cause we like your style,' he says, 'only you need*

science. Soon learn. You from the Smoke?'

So they took us to a Gents and got us cleaned up, and we was still limping, but we wasn't hurt all that bad, see, and they took us to a coach they had parked on some waste ground. And you should have seen who was on it. There's the Murphys, that bog-trotting lot out of Fyle Street, Billy Parrott and that shower that gets down in the Copa, and a mob out of Highbury.

And they reckon you can learn a mixture of karate and kungfu and that, and there's these pressure-points, see, which if you know them, you can put a man on his back. You can paralyse him, like for life, if you don't watch it. A little bloke like you, Kev, you could take on a couple of big sods. It's just like you got to know where to push in with your thumbs. And these two crack on you can learn it in two hours, enough anyway so you can use yourself.

So Arfer and me, we say we'll give it a oncer, 'cause they always have a coach, this lot. And they always have a good nosh at some transport caff afterwards. We got to meet them at a caff in the Holloway Road. Wonder when we'll see them two punks again.

Willy? Oh, he was waiting for us back of them lock-up garages, back of Camden Broadway. Daren't go in without us, see, case the Old Woman won't let him out with us again. Told the inspector he'd lost his ticket, got his name and address took. Letter came yesterday. British Rail. The old woman di'n't half create.

Judith Pascoe appended her initials to her first minute in her new grade. JDP Asst Sec. JP sounded like a magistrate, and no one outside Estabs need know she'd been christened Daisy after a great-aunt. Outside the Civil Service, Assistant Secretary sounded like an apprentice to the typing pool. Inside the corridors of influence it was something fruitier: the *pons asinorum* of the Administrative Grade—the first rank in which you might find yourself dealing direct with a minister.

Not that Judith Pascoe was sure that transfer and promotion had come entirely through merit. She had met Percy Mather at a joint working lunch over at Applied Arts, and she knew she'd made an involuntary conquest. Of course, it had to be a man in his fifties with yellow occlusion in the corners of his eyes. But Mather must be a power in the land, if he'd been able to get her moved within three months, not only to the Duchy, but right under his own thumb. It might be some time before the crucial thrust and parry came. She'd play that as it happened, when it happened, if it happened. In the meantime there was a backlog mountain here that looked promising to a candid careerist. Very different from Arts, where you had to let weeks elapse on principle before saying No to financial requests from provincial ballet companies, otherwise they thought they hadn't been looked at. Time had dragged in Wellington Terrace. But it wasn't going to drag here. Percy Mather hadn't made a decision for years—and didn't seem to mind what she cleared off his desk.

She closed a file three inches thick, was about to put it in the messenger's tray, then thought it might be an idea to drop it in personally on the addressee. She'd have to confront him sooner or later. He was a man she had been warned about—which was only one reason why he fascinated her. Moreover, there was a sense of embitterment in his minutes that tempted her to explore. When she tapped on his door, Peter Paul Whippletree was engaged not in the solution but in the composition of a crossword puzzle.

'Ah!'

One would have thought that he had been expecting her—in fact that he was her boss, not *vice versa*, and that she was a couple of minutes late: a young man refreshingly without respect of any kind. He did not uncross his ankles from the corner of his desk. There was even something agreeable — provided he did not overdo it — in his totally negative reaction to her femininity. She was brunette in her late twenties, trim, poised, with a hint that a different creature might be lurking somewhere under her academically styled spectacles. She knew precisely when to take these off; which was not this morning.

'You've got a better office than I have,' she said, taking in his direct view of Millbank, the grey ruffled river with gulls, his two Paul Nash prints and his own percolator bubbling at the ready. Assistant Principal sounded more imposing than Asst Sec, but it was only the lance-corporal's stripe of the First Division, and he ought to be ashamed of himself for not going up at least one in the time that he'd been here. She put him at about thirty, with a certain puerile eagerness, and to judge by the file she was carrying, he must have some inner reason for hiding his ability most of the time. This was good stuff.

'I've just come from PUSS,' she said.

'Dear old Percy.'

'Our Permanent Under-Secretary of State is impressed by your cockshy. He's asked me to clarify a few points.'

'About time. He sat on one of my files for two years. Which one is this?'

She could have quoted from memory, but looked down and read from the cover.

'*An examination in depth of alternative proposals for the suppression of football hooliganism.*'

'Suppression of football would of course be the surest.'

He got up to attend to his percolator.

'Have a coffee. Drop in and have one at this hour every morning. Have you met the sludge from the canteen yet? And how's Percy? Don't let me rock the boat for you.'

She blushed, with annoyance rather than embarrassment, and then was further furious with herself for letting it show.

'I don't know what you mean. Let's stick to soccer hooligans. And I *will* have a coffee, please.'

'If you need any tips on handling Percy, he's reasonably transparent, and I've been here longer than he has. Two days. Foundation member.'

'Thank you. I think I know the proper relationship with one's Under-Secretary.'

'Ah—but do you know enough about the improper one? Did you know that he is reputed to have active erogenous zones on the dimples of his elbows? Also, he can very easily be deflated—or do I mean deflowered?— well, anyway, de-erected. By—'

It was almost too much. But she had to establish that this sort of thing did not affect her.

'I'd be delighted to hear what you know about me,' she said, with firm self-discipline.

'Ah. There you have me. Some of the reports are a little slow coming through. I do know your academic side. Newnham. First in Part I English, didn't quite make it in Part II—but a top second is considered good enough for research these days. Hence your M. Litt—for a thesis on the Battle Songs of Theodolf von Hvin. Not entirely predictable for a greengrocer's daughter, even if she did come up through the North London Collegiate. But maybe it's only greengrocers' daughters who specialize in Early Norse these days.'

She was angry now—but determined not to give him the satisfaction of knowing it.

'You're not supposed to know any of that. Have you a private line to Estabs?'

'It pays to know one's enemy.'

'You're intent on making me that, are you?'

Whippletree went back to his desk and picked up the

sheet of squared paper on which he was compiling his crossword.

'Produce of mad stream badly cut here question mark. Far from true,' he read aloud.

'Amsterdam,' she replied at once. It was not only Arfer who did not need time for thought.

'That's obviously too easy.'

He drew a squiggly line through his tentative clue.

Kenworthy moved towards the door of the conference hall. September — and hot: but heavy curtains were drawn against the ceiling-high glass for an afternoon film-show.

'Your card, sir, please.'

The security guard came forward, not fawning, not expecting a delegate to be without his ID, but not prepared to be seen falling down on his job.

'Sorry, sir. Mr Kenworthy, isn't it? Good to see you again, sir.'

Kenworthy did not recognize him: some beat-basher who'd once seen him from a distance. Probably stood at the front door, keeping reporters away from the evidence, when he'd been with the Murder Squad. Kenworthy put his hand to his inside pocket, where he had Whippletree's letter.

'Mine's the next turn on the bill,' he said.

'Don't mind me, sir. They're all in there.'

'See you around. Look for a chance to buy you a pint.'

He moved into the hall. It was a Teacher Training College, Egham, overlooking the Thames Valley, high above Runnymede. A slit or two of sunshine escaped in from the greenery outside. Within shone the smoky beam of a projector. Hot bodies smelled stale in thick, unsuitable clothes.

On the screen a blown-up still from a two- or three-year-old news sequence showed a punch-up against a wire fence. Kenworthy had seen it once in a paper, could not remember where or when. It could have been an alarum in one of the inner-city affrays. A circle had been drawn round a boot that a willowy West Indian was putting into the ear of a fallen policeman. Then the scene changed to shipboard devastation: saloon upholstery ripped open, tables splintered, the panelling of a bar stove in.

'A Sealink ferry after the return crossing of disappointed England supporters.'

But then something more riveting: a grey, magnified urban scene. Albert Square, Manchester, just before the First War, judging from people and costumes: baggy trousers, raggy caps, thin-stemmed pipes, women in ankle-length drabness. The Town Hall was a menacing backdrop, the turn-of-century style of the Joe Lyons nostalgic. Who'd remember now what a Nippy was?

But this had never happened in Manchester. Even Peterloo had stopped short of this. Three tables had been set on a platform in the middle of the Square, on each table three kitchen chairs, on each chair a man, blindfolded, noosed to a single long gallows bar. And at the moment of exposure, the tables had just been toppled—by a platoon of British soldiers in service dress and puttees. The chairs were just free of the prisoners' feet. They were within a fraction of a second of their deaths—if the knots had been placed correctly. If they hadn't, they were going to choke on the ropes for twenty minutes or so.

Kenworthy wondered: how did you get nine men to stand meekly on nine chairs? Was it really so strong, the compulsion to behave with dignified conformity?

Someone laughed. Nervous reaction. The lights came on. Before any man moved his rump on his canvas chair, there was an eye-blinking pause. A chairman hoisted himself on to the apron of the stage.

'Needless to say, it hasn't come to that—yet,

gentlemen. May I add that that last scene did not take place in Manchester? But the incident *did* happen. It was said to be extremely persuasive.'

'It persuaded those nine,' someone said. 'May we ask where?'

'Salonika, nineteen-fifteen. Bulgarian partisans—I think. Somebody, anyway.'

Men were standing up, restoring circulation to numbed parts.

'Take five, then. Maybe after that, we've deserved ten. Has anyone seen the next attraction arrive?'

Kenworthy went forward to make himself known. It had all started with a phone call.

'Mr Kenworthy? P.P. Whippletree, here, Duchy of Axholme. I'm speaking on behalf of the Chancellor to ask you—'

Duchy of Axholme? Weren't they that ragtime bunch that the Opposition were currently doing their damnedest to crucify?

'Would you consider taking part in a conference that the Duchy is co-ordinating?'

What the hell could the Duchy be interested in that Kenworthy could help with?

'It's for Defence Chiefs, Senior Staff Officers, Heads of Government Departments and other interested bodies.'

They were going to give law and order another airing, then. No harm in playing along with that, meet a few new faces, a few old ones, earn an honest guinea or two. Doubtless it was comic relief that they wanted. That was why promoters of these things dragged Kenworthy in these days.

'The theme is *Population Management in cases of breakdown of the civil authority.*'

'Are you sure you've got hold of the right chap? I've never managed a population in my life. Nor have I ever known a civil authority break down.'

'Ah—but suppose it does?'

> '*Tomorrow after new young men,*
> *The Sergeant he must see,*
> *For things will all be over then*
> *Between the Queen and me.*'

'Housman,' P.P. Whippletree said.

'Correct.'

'I hesitate to contradict you, Mr Kenworthy, but we have a note on file that you spoke to the Forest Hill and Sydenham Rotary Club in nineteen forty-seven on your experiences in a German village, just before the war ended. Was it just after the Rhine Crossing?'

'Stone the crows! What sort of files do you keep in your department?'

'Nothing sinister, I assure you. But we do have a sort of rag-bag—'

'Nice to know where one belongs.'

It was true. In 1947, two years after the event, it had still seemed worth talking about. He had not been able to forget it. A Field Security Sergeant, he had been detached from his section to make the crossing on the Sappers' first pontoon, to contact his oppos in the airborne drop beyond the river, to attend to any viable problems before the main body arrived and consolidated. And Kenworthy, thanks to ramshackle communications, had got himself cut off. A long range young Nazi soldiers' patrol-group, sixteen- and seventeen-year-olds from a fanatical Cadet School on the plain, had hooked forward and besieged the village in which he happened to be. They had held up a whole British Army Corps. No one was keen on a wall of dead at this stage.

For four days Kenworthy had had to get and keep things organized for a population of some two hundred living in Frankish farmhouses that looked as if they had been clipped out of a Grimm scrapbook. It had in fact organized itself. The wealthiest local farmer had been machine-gunned with his family, trying to take cover in the fields. His larder was massively full and Kenworthy had laid on a rough and ready rationing system. People came and told tales about lesser hoards. The reluctant toed the line for fear of reprisals. Two wells were the only water-sources not suspected of corpse-contamination: a daily allowance was worked out, a distribution squad organized. The self-important village police chief was on the Allied *Wanted* list; his constable wasn't. Kenworthy watched with sardonic amusement while the *Schupo* locked his boss up in their single cell with unsmiling Teutonic obedience. The dough-faced imbecile even asked his own erstwhile captain for his name and occupation, before entering them laboriously in the station register.

Easy. Patriotism and blood-quickening political slogans moved nobody. Everywhere one saw unrelieved destruction. There was no spirit of Twilight of the Niebelungs about end-of-war Stapelfeld. They were used to doing what uniform told them to—even when it was worn by an enemy sergeant whose only armament was a .38 pistol. (Kenworthy was the only one who knew that his firing-pin was broken.) The only trouble came from French refugees from a forced-labour camp, who saw no reason for any Boche to survive. They got tanked-up from homemade hock found in the farm cellars. It was tempting to sympathize with the poor sods—but it had a hushing effect on Stapelfeld when he chucked them in the pound, alongside the unprotesting police captain.

Second Army eventually mopped up the Cadets. Kenworthy holstered his useless pistol and rode off with the last half-gallon in the tank of his motor-cycle to look for his mobile HQ—and be asked where the hell he had been. Happy days—

'Are you still there, Mr Kenworthy?'

P.P. Whippletree—

'Yes. I hardly think, you know, that my little exploit has much message for the contemporary world. North-Rhine Westphalia at the end of the war was hardly Toxteth or Moss Side.'

'The Chancellor thinks that the underlying principles might teach us something.'

Momentary silence. Kenworthy saw the bathos of being put up in front of combined Chiefs of Staff nearly forty years after so mild an event as a war with conventional weapons.

But Whippletree got him there. He told first one or two secondhand stories: how somebody had organized a village in the Burmese jungle, somebody else had set up a minor emirate, harem and all, in abandoned Nissen huts in Tunisia. Then he came to a band of British Prisoners of War, escaping when their camp had been overrun by Rokossovsky. They had trekked across Poland in 1946 with discipline and improvised logistics, whereas a camp of Central European *staatenlos* DPs, let loose after the front line had shattered their wire, had had to be rounded up again after devastating a landscape.

Why the difference? The difference between a purpose and a destination on the one hand, and the incohesion of despair on the other. But this audience leaped readily to xenophobia. *Bloody foreigners—*

Who were these delegates? Service Chiefs, Chiefs of Staff, Departmental Heads, Whippletree had said on the phone. It was possible to spot a mufti major-general, accustomed to say *Go and he goeth*. There was a man who might have been an observer from the Home Office. But these were not top-level planners. There were too many among them whom Kenworthy recognized from a different context—

The chairman called for questions. A beefy, fresh-faced young man stood up—that amazingly youthful sort that one saw being interviewed on the box as battalion commanders in Belfast.

'I'm sure we all listened with interest to Mr Kenworthy: low key, low profile. Could I ask him if he has any special message for this gathering?'

'Nobody has told me what this gathering is. I don't think I'm supposed to know—'

Laughter.

'Why do you really think you succeeded, Mr Kenworthy—in a breakdown situation that could have been extremely unfunny?'

'I cashed in on their habit of mind,' Kenworthy said. 'They were waiting to be told what to do.'

'And not one Nazi left among them? Not one bitter widow, sworn to take one with her? Not one vengeful old man who'd lost four mighty sons?'

Kenworthy sought for words. Did he know the answer himself? Had he at any moment been in danger? Hadn't he just followed his nose? He heard someone's voice come to his rescue: an attractive young lady, out of place in the company. The very sight of her made Kenworthy feel his age.

'Maybe there was something to be said, even on the edge of a battle, for a ray or two of common sense and goodwill.'

'I'd like him to tell me,' the lieutenant-colonel said, 'how to radiate goodwill and common sense in the Falls Road.'

But then the chairman was putting up the shutters, moving them off somewhere else. Kenworthy was aware of an apparent sixth-form schoolboy hovering.

'Thank you, Mr Kenworthy. Just what the Chancellor wanted. If you'd like to come and fill in an expense claim, I'll see you're not kept waiting for your cheque.'

'Ah.'

'Peter Paul Whippletree,' the schoolboy said. Maybe he was an undergraduate. And somebody else was hanging about for a chance to make herself known: the young lady who had come to his aid at question time.

'Judith Pascoe. Splendid, Mr Kenworthy. I hope you'll allow us to keep you on our books.'

'Books? I don't really know where I am, you know. You are—?'

'Duchy.'

'I'm afraid your Duchy's always been a bit of a mystery to me.'

'That's how we like it.'

'Then may I ask you: are you near enough to the Duke and Duchess to—'

'We don't run to a Duke. Only a Chancellor.'

'Could you on his behalf give me permission to sit in on the next item?'

He had noticed it on the agenda. *A Functional Grammar of Mass Hysteria.*

But she wagged a forefinger like a toy revolver.

'You know that's a naughty request. Classified matter. More than my job's worth!'

Sweet: she would have a Calvinist elder assessing her bedworthiness. But he knew that there was no point in pressing his request.

'I'll creep back home, then.'

CHAPTER 2

The next day a phone-call from the Faculty—from Bransby-Lowndes himself, the smooth operator.*

Kenworthy had known that sooner or later the 'Faculty', the special investigating team working direct for the Cabinet Office, would be calling him out again. He

* See *The Asking Price*

knew he'd be disappointed if they didn't — but he wasn't going to play all that easy to get. Because he had an idea that they wouldn't remember his existence again until they were stuck — or had ballsed something up.

'Were you likely to be dropping round this way in the near future?' Bransby-Lowndes, liaison officer, asked him.

'No.'

'Only we'd rather like to hear your impressions of yesterday.'

'Yesterday?'

'We hear you were preaching to the unconvertible, Egham way.'

'Oh, that —'

'Yes, that. You don't think you got there by accident, do you?'

'Or because of any special aptitude, I suppose?'

Bransby-Lowndes clicked his tongue.

'Stop pretending to bristle, Simon. You're not good at it. And we are anxious to hear your impressions. Today, rather than tomorrow.'

'Impressions?'

'Of the Duchy.'

'If you'd told me why I was going, I'd have known what to look for.'

'Then you'd have looked too hard. And you'd have been seen to be looking. Can we say two o'clock? No: make that half past three. I'm out to lunch.'

'Don't tell me,' Kenworthy said. 'There's no Duke.'

'No — but there's a Chancellor. At present Lord Downes. And so that some one can account to the Commons, there's a Vice-Chancellor, Hersholt, Member for Manchester Didsbury. He wouldn't be there yesterday. His permanent staff will have seen to that. They have had long expertise at embarrassing their masters. That's how many of them come to be there.'

'How's that?'

'Here's an extract from Hansard that will show you how it all started.' It was an off-print, dated in the 1960's.

MR PHILIP CORNARD asked the Prime Minister the purpose of the newly established Duchy of Axholme.

THE PRIME MINISTER: Axholme is a former island reclaimed from the North Lincolnshire Fens in the seventeenth century. This small new department has been created to tidy up certain anomalies in the administration of Crown lands in that area.

MR CORNARD: Is this not an irresponsible proliferation of bureaucracy at a time when the country has been promised retrenchment in Civil Service numbers?

THE PRIME MINISTER: In point of fact, with a total staff of thirty-six, this is a very small department. Every vacancy has been filled by transfer from other departments and most of those transferred are already close to retirement. The tasks entrusted to them are complex but finite. It is largely a question of ambiguous titles to parcels of farmland, some of which have gone unresolved since the Civil War. It is confidently expected that the Duchy will have wound up its own reason for existence within the working lifetime of its present staff.

'In point of fact,' Bransby-Lowndes explained, 'this was an astute device whereby an incoming government got rid of some of its most embarrassing deadwood. The foundation staff of the new Duchy consisted of two categories—'

'To begin with, useless buggers,' Forrester said.

Bransby-Lowndes assumed his most refined murderous look.

'And those who were so bad at manipulating inexperienced ministers that they got caught out at it.'

'*Yes, Minister*,' Kenworthy suggested.

'Except that this was not comic. There are ways in which an unscrupulous head of department can make life hell for an elected chief whose policies don't suit him. He can delay projects pending. He can keep quiet about snags. He can set up bad PR. He can provide woozy answers to parliamentary questions. In extreme cases, he can get rid of him. If you remember, Caudwell of Clee was head of the Civil Service Department at this time.'

'Never heard of him,' Kenworthy said, with provocative honesty.

'A strong character, and one who knew more ropes than there were in the rigging. The Duchy of Axholme was his baby. He dug up this mess of Pre-Commonwealth titles in the Grimsby and Barton-on-Humber hinterland, and it was reckoned that his three dozen hand-chosen undesirables would wallow about in them for the rest of their government service. It was a prime mixture of the dangerously inept and the positively poisonous. Each of them was pushed up a grade on transfer. They even gained on pension, so no one complained. And needless to say there were honours galore: CVOs. CBs, even an acute case of KCB. It cost the government practically nothing.'

Bransby-Lowndes sat back to ensure that he was being appreciated. Forrester, behind a desk that was stacked rather than littered with work, would have a few key additions to the story when Bransby-Lowndes had finished and gone. They were conferring in Forrester's office because Bransby-Lowndes would not countenance Kenworthy's pipe in his own.

'Now look at this. A Hansard for six years later.'

MR BASIL JONES (Fishguard Hamlets): Will the Prime Minister inform the House of the present administrative strength of the Chancelry of the Duchy of Axholme?

THE PRIME MINISTER: At the moment the number stands at 2,007 of whom 120 in clerical grades are temporary or part-time appointments.

MR JONES: May I refer the Prime Minister to his predecessor's reply of six years ago? What has happened to the finite life of this totally unnecessary and recklessly extravagant department? Is a 5,500 per cent increase in staff considered necessary in order to secure evictions that are unlikely to be held up by the courts?

'Rather a nasty one that, Bransby-Lowndes said. 'An over-zealous Chancellor, grossly misled by his Permanent Secretary, tried to dispossess a family who had had tenure for four generations. Thrown out on Appeal with an acrid *envoi* from the Master of the Rolls.'

THE PRIME MINISTER: The initial role of the Duchy has now been fulfilled. The Duchy is being developed as a Ministry of Contingency Planning, and my Right Honourable Friend the Chancellor will be informing the House from time to time of its progress. In particular, we hope that pressure will be taken off the Central Policy Review Staff, popularly known, I believe, as the think tank. They will then be able to devote themselves to more pressing issues.

AN OPPOSITION MEMBER: Pity.

MR JONES: May we be given examples of questions entrusted to the Duchy?

THE PRIME MINISTER: It is early days for that, sir.

'You can see what had happened, Kenworthy. Not only had there been this frightful rocket from the Master of the Rolls, the Duchy had expanded for the very reason that had brought it into existence in the first place.'

'More useless buggers?'

Bransby-Lowndes winced.

'If we must use such terms. I fear there was a surfeit of

suitable qualified recruits, not only at Administrative level, but also Executive Officers, clerks, messengers and paper-keepers. I am afraid that Ministers—and more than one departmental head—once the opportunities were appreciated, took advantage of the chance to off-load. Bolshies, subordinates who knew too much, chronic procrastinators, blunderers and the situation-prone all made their way down to Millbank. So something had to be found for them to do. What more innocuous than working on long-winded plans for improbable emergencies? After all, it is open to any government to reject their advice.'

'Fine. I am sure that in a national context the expenditure was well justified. It amounted to shunting inefficiency into sidings.'

'But it doesn't stop there, Simon. What the founders of the Duchy did not allow for was the Pygmalion element: the chance that it might develop a life of its own. The Duchy was conceived as a safe way of canalizing wasted time. A few reports have been submitted—and shelved. Some were commissioned by the government of the day—like a working paper on *Stray Dogs*, for example. Some have been thought up by cheerful Chancellors, shortly after their appointment. But I regret to say that many have been initiated internally by heads of branch who thoroughly understood their Northcote Parkinson.'

Bransby-Lowndes changed his posture in his chair, a signal that the tone of his revelations was about to change. He wanted a little less cynicism, if you please, a little more respectful attention from Messrs Forrester and Kenworthy.

'This is serious. For the last two and a half years or so, someone in the Duchy has had a curious obsession with civil unrest in all its manifestations. Casual disorder, organized disorder—even football hooliganism. That was the subject of a major working paper, produced as far as

one can see on his own initiative, by a particularly un-
savoury whippersnapper called Whippletree. Actually,
he's not as young as he looks and he's been an Assistant
Principal in the Duchy since Day One. He made a
frightful bounder of himself on his first appointment to
another ministry.'

'I met him yesterday.'

'Yes. He was in on that act. And for all his capering,
Whippletree has a brain. He passed with phenomenal
high marks for Foreign Service entry, but was rejected on
personality. Now we all know that the police and the
services have plans in their pigeonholes for dealing with
serious riots. That's one of their reasons for existing.
There have been controversial courses at the Staff
College, Camberley — and believe me, they would be a
damned sight more controversial if the public knew some
of the exercises that have been carried out. That aspect
doesn't worry me. If trouble does come — and we've had a
taste of it in Brixton, Toxteth and Moss Side — these
people will be looked to to settle it. So they are entitled to
examine it from hypothetical angles.'

Bransby-Lowndes was suave and intelligent. He saw
deeply enough into many problems to know not to make
them his concern. But he was committed to this one.

'Then we discovered — never mind how — the old need-
to know rule — that the Duchy of Axholme had been
working on parallel lines. And just for once, it wasn't with
that amateurish abandon that typifies most of their work.
This was a scientific, exhaustive, well-developed
reactionary plan. It could be pulled out of the drawer and
presented to any government with its back to the
wall — and no time to think. Nobody knows who was
really responsible. Whippletree certainly worked on some
facets of it, but the underlying genius remains a mystery.
Oh, there's been a scapegoat. There had to be. A man
called Bessemer, a head of section, was ripe for a Mental

Home anyway, and has been persuaded to go into one. His place has been taken by a young woman of promise called Pascoe, a veritable porcupine of integrity. She has been given no in-depth briefing about the troubles preceding her. Her job is to bring her Section back to useful occupations—or, at least, harmless ones.'

'You mean that a man has been put away so that an erring department can be pulled back to its feet?'

There were times when Bransby-Lowndes seemed devoid of compassion. The sequestered Bessemer did not worry him at all.

'It was always touch and go with Bessemer. No injustice there, I think. He's not the only labile type in the Duchy. And is there any wonder?'

'But is the danger really so great?'

'Are unofficial vigilantes dangerous? Powerful ones? Who are assumed to have govenment support? There's probably more resentment smouldering in the Duchy than in any government building in the kingdom. And civil commotion is just waiting to be provoked: racism, unemployment, industrial unrest, tower blocks, crummy housing estates, poverty, festering aggression—So let it boil over; then step in and restore order. Draconian counter-measures.'

'It wouldn't work,' Kenworthy said.

'No? Cromwell failed ultimately. But we don't want a Second Protectorate, do we? Even for a month or two?'

'Is it as bad as that?'

'You spoke yesterday at a conference: an information exchange, if you like. It was very different from what had been orginally planned. It was going to be a full-scale operational planning session, an introduction of certain gentlemen to each other. You saw who was there. Fortunately the original agenda was spotted by a watch-dog in the Duchy, an on-the-ball Deputy Secretary called Burton. He watered it down—your turn was part of the water-ration—sent out his new agenda to the original invitation list. To see what might happen. I think a lot of men went home from Egham puzzled and disappointed.'

There followed a short but ponderous silence. Bransby-Lowndes had not altogether made it sound real. Picturesque narrative was not where his gifts lay. These things did not belong to his elegant voice, his delicate frame, the cut of his suit. But that was the dangerous refuge of the quietist: *it can't happen here.*

It mustn't happen here. There had to be men capable of imagining what it would be like if it did. That was what intelligence services were for.

'Do you seriously think anyone is going to try?' Kenworthy asked.

'Half the cabinet do—that's more to the point than anything I think. So *your* job—'

'Steady on. I haven't got a job. I came in and helped you out once—'

'I know we can't conscript you. And it would be a bore having to appeal to your nobler nature.'

'I haven't one.'

'Don't *you* be a bore, Simon.'

'All right. I won't. My job is to infiltrate.'

'No. You've done all the infiltrating you're going to. There'd be men at Egham surprised to see you there. But they accepted you at your face-value: a replacement lecturer. You weren't even allowed to sit in on other items: a neat thought. Something had gone wrong. No one knew what. You were part of the cover-up—an innocent part of it. And it will be known that you've come to this office. All right—you *would* come, wouldn't you? Let's leave it at that. Let's push it no further.'

'For fear they give up?'

'There's no chance of that. There are men with too much to gain—and only one way of gaining it. You know who they are. You saw them. So now tell us.'

Once or twice, Kenworthy had seen Bransby-Lowndes's professionally groomed nonchalance dissolve, its place taken by almost comically naïve enthusiasm. It was usually because he hoped that within the next few seconds, something was going to be confirmed that he had forecast. That mood was on him now.

'Partly it was the dog-that-didn't-bark syndrome,' Kenworthy said. 'Not who was there, but who wasn't.'

'And who wasn't?'

'MI5. Special Branch. Not a soul I knew from the security services. Of course, I know there have been changes. All the same—'

'You're right, of course. They weren't on the distribution list. They wouldn't be. They're outside this exercise.'

'We have too many intelligence services by half in this country,' Kenworthy said. 'And they're not doing—'

He digressed on a favourite theme: proliferation and no accountability. Forrester and Bransby-Lowndes allowed him the luxury: for a short time.

'Now tell us who *was* there.'

Kenworthy looked pointedly at Forrester, and began ticking off names on his fingers.

'Walter Kershaw, D.D. Bragg, Sam Tyrrell, Dykes, Bellamy, Barraclough, Richardson—I counted a dozen retired Yard men.'

Forrester nodded. He knew them. He knew why they upset Kenworthy. Forrester had always been clean at the Yard. Like Kenworthy, he'd had nothing to fear when Sir Robert Mark had started pitching in. But he had never taken things to heart as Kenworthy had. He had kept his nose well wiped, had got on with his job, not cared about others—and here he was.

About Kenworthy there had always been some mystery. There had been something monstrous that he had resented—that he had never ceased to resent. It had not even been rumoured what it was: some massive injustice that he had known about, perhaps, some internal barricade that had been put up to save somebody's skin; something he had wanted to do something about himself, but that had proved too big for him. It had come near to making him physically ill. Colleagues close to him knew that. In the end he had come out voluntarily, a little, not too long, before this time. Because he could not stand the stink, men knew. But they did not know which stink. And the danger signs always went out from Kenworthy if the conversation veered towards the point at which some trespasser might risk asking him outright.

His anger was rising now: one might have thought it was Bransby-Lowndes or Forrester who had offended him.

'I never held with the way it was done. When a man of the rank of Commander was sent to gaol—and Mark was threatening to have every plainclothes officer back on the beat—there were hundreds, *hundreds*, as you know, Forrester, of officers who were given the chance to resign, rather than face further investigation. What sort of way was that of setting about it? Every single one should have been chased to his ruin, no matter what it cost, no matter what sort of wreck it left behind. Now it's being suggested that the sting was taken out of *Countryman*. It should be unthinkable that men should have to suggest that.'

And he began the count on his fingers again.

'Walter Kershaw, D.D. Bragg, Sam Tyrrell, Dykes, Bellamy, Barraclough—They were all there yesterday.'

'Not on the payroll of the Duchy. You know what they are? They are Natsecure—'

'Nazi Corps?'

'Sorry, Simon. That joke has already been made. Natsecure is a new private security agency, uniformed, barely off the ground yet. Its cap-badge is suggestively similar to the official portcullis. Its board of directors was present yesterday at Egham—with the exception of its chairman.'

Kenworthy waited for it.

'Cawthorne.'

Kenworthy looked sick with disgust.

'So we thought you'd be interested.'

'Is the Duchy running Natsecure, or is Natsecure running the Duchy?'

'It will be interesting to find out.'

'I expect you've got a run-down of the Duchy—a family-tree of their organization? Who ostensibly does what?'

'Routine. You shall have a copy before you leave.'

'Plus the notes that Forrester will have made about what holes they all crawled out of.'

'Likewise.'

'I'll be in touch.'

CHAPTER 3

Cor, talk about a bleeding rip-off. There's Arf and me thinking we're going to learn suffink, and when we goes to this caff in Holloway, Tuesday, see, the tart behind the counter, she says if we're Finsbury fans we've got to go to Jimmy Maddock's, behind the Paki restaurant.

I should bleeding cocoa. Join Jimmy's bleeding Boys' Club? Me and Arfer poncing about in PE shorts, jogging in Kenwood, Satday afternoons? Then Jimmy starts in on us because we've brought nothing to change into. I says screw this, and we're just going to piss off out of it when this other bloke comes in, what we run into in Gorleston, and he says if anybody wants to see Finsbury play Parkeston on Friday night, floodlit and that, there'll be a coach outside the Enkel Arms. Only nobody's got to carry

*no weapons. Like, though a few pebbles or marbles in our
pockets could come in handy.*

So we hung about.

'Yes, Mr Mather, I'll come up.'

The fourth time in three days. PUSS, Mr Mather, had
all the Study Groups in his charge, each managed by an
Assistant Secretary. As far as she could gather from what
talk she had had with them, the heads of the other groups
did not set eyes on Percy once in a blue moon. They got
their orders in his fastidious calligraphy and kept him
informed in endless ricochets of files, which he returned
to them at long intervals, usually calling for some trivial
amendment. Though reluctant to dictate, he had a habit
of getting his own way over semi-colons. It was a wonder
anything ever got back to the department that had asked
for it. Perhaps nothing ever did.

But Mather was always sending for her. At first she
thought it might be because she was new in the job, and
he wanted her on the right lines from the start. But he
never got down to revealing what and where the lines
were. He would pick up something she'd passed him a
fortnight ago. Say *The Fouling of Footpaths by
Domesticated Animals: a comparison of regional bye-
laws.* He would seize upon some paragraph on the second
page, begin to mumble something, degenerate into
inaudibility, then look up from the paper and away from
her.

'But who am I to know better than the man who has
done the work? From whose pen is this, Miss Pascoe?'

'Mr Whippletree's.'

'Indeed?'

He would look at her and dare to smile, until she
smiled back at him, and then he would have to look away.
If ever she moved in close enough for him to catch her
perfume, his consternation was cruel to witness.

She had been certain, after their working meeting at Applied Arts, that it was he who had engineered her transfer here. He had seemed a different creature on that committee. Perhaps getting away from his own premises had enlivened him. Could she believe now that he was a puller of strings? He might now and then stretch out his hand towards one, introspective, alone and unwatched. But he'd withdraw it again before it bit him. He hadn't exactly looked as if he was going to proposition her that day at Arts. Now it was a prospect that existed only on the fringes of his fantasy. Judith Pascoe felt safe with Percy Mather. She considered herself liberated from moral bigotry, but there were such things as æsthetic considerations, and the thought of Percy in bed was grotesque.

Percy got up and walked round to his window, which commanded the same view as Whippletree's, only from a higher level, and largely obscured by a balustrade encrusted with pigeon droppings.

'South Bank — metaphysical poets — pestilential, pestilential — '

He had a habit, when on the verge of some pronouncement of which he felt unsure, of muttering disconnected trigger-words, as if the volcano of his mind were experimenting with a handful of gravel before letting fly with the main pay-load.

'Do you care for *lamproie bordelaise*, Miss Pascoe?'

'Not to distraction,' she said.

'Pity.'

He took his eyes off her and concentrated soulfully on the bird-shit.

'Lamprey? Ortolans, perhaps — ? Nettles — ? No, that's *orties*, isn't it? No obstacle. No obstacle.'

He came back to her.

'No obstacle, Miss Pascoe. Other things on the menu. I had thought, if I wouldn't be imposing upon you — a quiet little dinner. Bentley's, perhaps. The Pescatori—'

'That would be wonderful, Mr Mather.'

She wondered how she would be able to sit for an hour an a half through a conversation like a Max Ernst *collage*, went thoughtfully back to her room, pondering with an element of realism about the stack of bloody rubbish that was waiting on her desk.

Ah well: it was coffee time. She could always go down and bait Whippletree. She was beginning to find Whippletree oddly astringent.

'Sounds like a ring of swans?' he asked her this morning.

'Cygnet or signet—according to the cross-lights.'

'Two related clues in this puzzle. That always chuffs the editor. How about: Not a way of getting down in the Thames Valley?'

'Swan-upping.'

'You're smart.'

'And you're obviously wasted here.'

'Who isn't?'

He got up to attend to the coffee. He had oscillating enthusiasms. At the moment it had to be Guatemalan.

'Guess what, Peter Paul. I'm asked out for a discreet meal. By PUSS. He's offered me lamprey.'

It was some seconds before he turned back to face her. The news had upset him, which tickled her. By God, he was jealous. There hadn't been much artificiality between JDP and PPW in the last week or two. He came back with the cups, smiling naturally. Whippletree was resilient.

'In that case, someone ought to warn you. You know how Percy got here in the first place? Why he was chucked out of Industrial Relations?'

'He thought they were his sisters and his cousins and his aunts?' she said, hopelessly inept. She hated not being a true match for PP.

'No. He got the entire typing pool with child. Twenty-seven of them. Either during or shortly after an office party.'

'Thank's for the tip. I'll take precautions.'

'Don't be so bloody disgusting,' he said.

He *was* jealous.

'I promise to avoid a surfeit of his lamprey,' she said.

That was better.

CHAPTER 4

Kenworthy was soon absorbed in the organizational breakdown of the Duchy. It was a copious file, extending down to temporary clerical assistants. Forrester had appended his notes on individuals. And so had some of his minions. There were footnotes here and there that read a little subtly for Forrester's pen.

As a rough and ready visual guide, names were either heavily underlined in blue, to signify transferred for *incompetence*, with a triple scoring for Foundation Members; or in red, denoting *transferred for subversion, real or imagined*.

Thus Sir Henry Woodcroft, Permanent Secretary, on whose shoulders the administration and welfare of the entire Duchy rested, had come here on promotion from a Deputy Secretaryship at the Home Office for what was clearly chronic, pervasive and incorrigible laziness. Not only was he said to be averse to any effort, mental or physical, on his own part, but *took it unkindly in those around or subordinated to him, fearing and resenting any show of energy, enthusiasm, conscience or ambition in others*. Sir Henry's tangential contact with material life was absorbed in his collection of 'English' silver, almost exclusively that of the Huguenot craftsmen who came to this country following the Revocation of the Edict of

Nantes in 1685. Apparently he assumed that men and women of all walks of life were acquainted with the techniques and terminology of his hobby: the conversation invariably turned to *chinoiseries* and *cut-card work*, no matter what subject was under formal review. The writer of the notes wondered whether it was coincidence or someone's sense of the appropriate that had set him up in the Duchy, where most of the original problems of land-tenure stemmed from that same period as did Woodcroft's silver.

His two Deputy Secretaries, Thompson and Burton, were not underlined. This gave them no greater clearance than that nothing to their detriment had so far been traced. They both dated from the second phase of the Duchy's existence, and it seemed likely that it was one or both of them who saw to it that the office was kept in a state to do any work at all. J.F. Burton was the one who had spotted the sinister intent of the Egham conference and had substituted the less vicious agenda. He was known to disrespectful juniors as Killer Burton.

Many of the heads of branches, mostly Permanent Under-Secretaries, had taken up their appointments within the last two or three years, as Foundation Members were falling away through natural retirement. Kenworthy worked his way down to Percival Mather, over-all manager of the Investigating Units and PUSS over J. Pascoe and P.P. Whippletree. Mather had been one of the first to come to the new office in Millbank, missing Foundation Membership by only forty-eight hours. (Apparently great weight was laid by some on trifling differences in seniority.) Even the most damning reports on Mather seemed to have been couched in sympathetic language. *A quick and incisive brain impeded by agonizing personal diffidence. Has been known to become totally incoherent under moderate stress. Grasps intricate problems and quickly evaluates solutions, but does not inspire loyalty in subordinates, except from workaholics and sycophants.* Mather was also a heart-case and had closely missed premature retirement some years ago after a medical board.

His kingdom consisted of five Study Groups, which actually performed the root-and-crop part of the Duchy's planning role:

I INDUSTRIAL:

(Undoubtedly strongly suspect by Unions and CBI alike, and treading on the heels of the Department of Employment.)

II SCIENCE AND MEDICINE:

(If Mather and his Asst Sec. had their wits about them, they would not be in competition with professional bodies that knew what they were about.)

III POPULACE:

(The Pascoe/Whippletree Unit)

IV PARLIAMENTARY:

(Presumably a euphemism for Political. But any government that risked using such a unit for party-political advantage would surely want something more robust than Mather's backside sitting on the crater.)

V EXTERNAL:

(Inquiries falling outside the UK. Liaison with MI6?)

The odd thing about Study Group III was how relatively free from besmirchings its personnel seemed to be — Whippletree apart. It began to look as if, from somebody's point of view, Unit III was intended to be efficient. With the perpetual exception of Whippletree, there was no reservation recorded against any member of it.

Judith Pascoe was noted as having a first-rate academic record and to have shown up outstanding papers in the competitive entry. Her spell at the Ministry of Applied Arts was characterised as *orthodox and competent but unscintillating.* Whippletree's immediate superiors were A.L. Grace, Senior Principal, and M.C. Tovey and E. Greenaway, Principals, about whom nothing was appended that was not in the pattern of good-living, compliant, promising and career-orientated public servants. And this pyramid, of which Whippletree would clearly be the fetcher-and-carrier, controlled the actual Study Group, who seemed equally free from any kind of objection. There were a dozen of them, including four women, and at least half of them had been direct entrants on first appointment. Again, it seemed as if someone had been determined to have new, well oxygenated blood flowing in free, uncrippled limbs. Were one to judge the Chancelry of the Duchy of Axholme by Study Group III (Populace) one might gain a very different impression from that given by Bransby-Lowndes in his overall sketch.

Except for Whippletree.

How, Kenworthy wondered, did Whippletree's immediate colleagues get on with him? What, as the saying went, could they make of him? Or was he simply left to get on with himself? Whippletree's name in the charts was underlined by the maximum three bars—probably drawn by Forrester's own fierce pencil, the grain of his desk showing up through the paper.

Whippletree was *unpunctual, provocatively slovenly in turnout, disrespectful of authority, rarely bothered to hide his contempt for the few assignments that could be entrusted to him.* These were gems from reports on his first year in his first appointment—before he had qualified for the Duchy. He had been sent for and talked to in approved house-masterly fashion about what was and what was not considered seemly deportment in a servant of the Crown. He was as unpopular with his co-equals as he was with those mentors who stubbornly tried to see hope for him. He suffered from *an intellectual arrogance* which made it *distasteful for anyone to share an office with him.* He was *openly and scathingly sceptical of the aims and purpose of his department.* He poured monotonous (and, Kenworthy imagined, trenchant) scorn on the efforts of any colleague he believed to be prompted by altruism, faith in received opinions or any kind of diligence other than that permissible for the relief of boredom. He himself achieved this latter by setting one crossword a week for a prestigious daily, a talent which he had been exercising since he was a sixth-form prodigy.

Moreover, as soon as he had occupied an executive desk long enough to learn where perversion could be most wickedly effective, he had developed a reputation as an irresponsible practical joker. When statistics were required with desperate urgency to back up a Minister against a Supplementary Question, the vital file went unaccountably missing. Visiting delegations from opposing sides of industry arrived to find their conference-rooms double-booked. When the Minister came for a slumming lunch in *hoi polloi's* canteen, an unexplained power failure made a catastrophe of the lunch.

The culmination was a visit by expressionless men with big eyebrows from beyond the Iron Curtain who, in an orgasm of détente, were being given an inside view of democracy. Someone—and Whippletree was circumstantially as well as temperamentally suspect—had affixed Clingfoil under the lavatory seats in the Private Office suite. There were one or two minor catastrophes for men who omitted to raise the seat, and a major one for a visitor who actually sat on it: a fundamental change of clothing had to be fetched from an Embassy.

Although Whippletree was only an Executive Officer (an entry grade for which A-Levels would have been adequate) he was pitchforked into the higher reaches and sent to the Duchy to consider the twentieth-century future of farmhouses erected by Roundheads on Cavalier pastures. It was not recorded what direct contact, if any, Whippletree ever had with Sir Henry.

There were still a large number of branches and officials to be looked at, but Kenworthy was conscious of having reached absorption point with mimeographed paper. He leafed over a thumbful of paper and applied himself to Security.

It was a lowly branch, an offshoot of Establishment, and the name of B.S. Iliffe, Higher Executive Officer, seemed to ring some sort of bell.

ILIFFE, Bernard Sykes; Age 57, Ex Chief Inspector, Met; Uniformed Branch. interrupted by a period as Inspector (Traffic) at NSY. Voluntary early retirement, before Yard purges. Reason given, domestic débâcle over unsocial hours, appears genuine. Uneventful career, undistinguished in any direction.

Friday afternoon: the Duchy would be doing little more than sealing down its hatches for the weekend. On Monday, Kenworthy would start. He must decide his point of entry. And on the principle of when in doubt tell the truth (or as much of it as is credible) he came down in favour of the approach direct. He scribbled down four names in order of preference.

Whippletree.

Pascoe.

Mather.

Iliffe.

CHAPTER 5

What to wear for a man who had better remain impressed, though there had to be no hint of come-hither? Judith Pascoe surveyed her wardrobe with a sense, not entirely unfamiliar, of dismay. It was not that she had ever been afraid, since she had been earning, of an occasional spending bout. The basic trouble was that she had always been in some doubt where she belonged. Now — not for the first time, but it had better be the last — she came to the sad but unsurprising conclusion that dual-purpose overlapped dangerously with neither-here-nor-there. She had to have done with gap-bridging. Now in the end it had to be her two-piece suit: the first that had occurred to her, and that she had rejected. Black velvet jacket and skirt, white frilly blouse. She could perhaps have looked formal enough in a trouser-suit; but she felt certain that Percy's preferences would be classical. And glasses. He had never seen her without. Tonight would not be the occasion.

She arranged to meet him Chez Festubert. He had apologized profusely for not coming to fetch her from her flat, but he had some late office conference. When she came in, he was standing at the bar in conversation with a man to whom she thought at first he was about to introduce her. But the stranger moved away as soon as she appeared. Percy seemed to be a connoisseur of sherry. She judged a Martini safe for herself. She felt as nervous, wanted to kick herself for it, as an undergraduate at her first Principal's bun-fight.

Sipping on after they had given their order, Percy was still in his stage of kaleidoscopic conversational knock-up.

'Lincolnshire — levity — leveret — Lincolnshire poachers—'

She tried to rescue him by a slam-down change of subject.

'Did you watch *Lear* on TV?'

'Getting the Globe into the box seems like trying to cube the sphere,' he said.

Excogitated, and he would not have got it out at all if he had not said it before many times. But after he had managed one finite sentence, others followed. They continued even after they had been called to their table.

'Mustn't talk shop. Been telling myself all day, no shop tonight. But I have to say this, Miss Pascoe—'

'Judith—'

'Judith, ah, Judith.'

But he did not invite her to drop the Mr. It had nothing to do with pomposity.

'I have to say this, have to ask you. The Duchy? Less melancholy than you feared, perhaps?'

'Oh yes, I'm enjoying myself very much.'

'The trouble is, our reputation. Dies hard. There was a time when if you were hand-picked for the Duchy, you asked yourself what you'd done. If you didn't know only too well.'

'I never thought for a moment—'

'It was like that in the old days. That's what we were for. There are still a few of the originals left. You'll find most of them now in Axholme branch. That's where they've coagulated. You must have asked yourself what they do in Axholme branch?'

'I take it for granted it's residual.'

'Residual. Good word. For people and their objectives. And sediment. Nothing much left for them to worry about now in Axholme branch, except ownership of a few fences: which side of the rails the posts ought to be on. They can go on hammering at that till they've all been

given their marble clocks. But that isn't the Duchy any
more. Some of us are determined it shan't be.'

Had he really persuaded himself that he himself hadn't
been deliberately marooned on Millbank?

'Some government soon is going to thank God that we
are here and have been pegging away at things.'

She took a discreet little look about the room. Wasn't
he talking just a trifle too loudly in his precariously
acquired confidence? What would eavesdroppers make of
this stuff?

'One more thing, and after that, no more shop, I
promise you. But I must say this. By our very nature, life
is getting more dangerous for us — dangerous for you,
too — and this is something you must know. You must
know for certain where you stand. Take Whippletree.
This new project of his. Needless to say, you're keeping a
diplomatic eye on what he's drafting?'

Peter Paul seemed to have a new project every few
minutes. She was not sure which one Percy knew — or
thought he knew — about.

'*A study in depth of the weighting of popular Opinion
Polls.* Has he really got such an impeccable source of
interviewers' records?'

Had he? She did not even know that the topic had
crossed Whippletree's mind. So how could Percy know?
Maybe it was old stuff that Percy only thought was new.
That would figure. But she'd better have a firm word
with Whippletree about Assistant Principals, Assistant
Secretaries and the proper bond of professional etiquette.

'Don't have to tell you where the dangers lie. Could
bring a government down — if not this, the next. Could
produce a dichotomy in any party. End of all stability.
And it's the press that wields these bludgeons. Fleet Street
will mass to kill.'

There was life in Percy's cholesterol-clouded eyes as if
they were embers catching a stray puff from broken bellows.

'Want you to know—he has my backing. Whippletree. As long as his case is sound. And he won't put it up if it isn't, not Whippletree. Boy's a perfectionist. And I'll back him. You need to know that—I'll back him.'

An over-wined diner came back from the lavatory, lurching against their table. Percy's consommé quivered but did not spill. A crust of roll fell to the floor. The drunk attempted to retrieve it, put it back on a corner of the table. The head waiter removed it, brought a fresh basket.

'So I hope you'll back him too. Without letting him think you're trying to run his work for him. Man-management, they call this sort of thing. Of course, I mean, this is only if you believe in it yourself.'

She was beginning to realize keenly that she did need something to believe in.

'That way, you'll escape Axholme branch,' he said. 'I know it's coming up. Franceys is going. And Burton might try to move you sideways if he doubts your strength.'

'I'll back Whippletree.'

'That's what I hoped to hear you say.'

And then he kept his promise and they stayed a mile away from any reminder that they worked under the same roof. Once he had unburdened his mind of what had required rehearsal, he developed not only a new fluency, but positive wit and charm—not without creating the assurance that he was the one who was being enchanted; and that he was getting more used to her physical nearness. He really was something of a dear.

They moved away from their table for coffee, and he insisted that she should learn the distinction of Armagnac over Cognac. When he finally stood up for her to go and fetch her coat, she was struck by how fragile he looked. He seemed momentarily quite absent. She asked him if he was feeling unwell.

'Please forgive me. My thoughts were aeons away. I hope I do not seem absolutely decrepit.'

He put a hand on her elbow, and she felt for an instant as if he were leaning on her for support. When she came back from the cloakroom, she was without her glasses. He had earned a reward; she was not quite sure why.

He insisted on a taxi for her up to Highgate, and on accompanying her. A flat in one of the sprawling Victorian redbricks in Bishopswood Road had been one of the perks that she felt that her promotion had justified. (Applied Arts had never seemed to belong outside bedsitland.) Percy did not talk much during the ride — or, at least, his conversation got trapped into one of its choppier gullies. Was he recoiling before a fresh hurdle? Surely he was not going to make a pass at her? What fashion might that take, with Percy?

Again she thought how ill he looked. When the cab pulled up, she asked him as a matter of form whether he would like to come in for a nightcap. (Form? The gap between Percy's world and the one in which she had grown out of being a greengrocer's daughter was so wide that she sometimes wondered whether it was safe to make any assumptions at all.)

'I would love to come in. Especially if you run to a drop of brandy — or any spirits except gin. To tell you the truth, I don't feel a hundred per cent myself.'

He took her arm as she showed him which pavement and which gate. He seemed to be in danger of falling.

CHAPTER 6

There were to be reasons why Geoff would not share their later exploits with Dud and Kev, but the narrative built up in his mind as of habit.

Cor, talk about shit on a blanket, getting shut of that bleeding Willy was like trying to pull one of your own choppers out. 'Cause Arfer and me knew that this bloke what got the coach up wouldn't want no nippers about.

So Arfer sends Willy home, see, 'cause he'd come out without his bog-rolls, only Willy won't go back for them and starts to give cheek, so Arfer fetches him one, and this old girl, she starts on that ain't no way to treat a kid, so Arf and me has to lean on her a bit, and she's in a thin shit, 'cause she thinks it's a mugging. And arter she's pissed off, and we've done falling about laughing, we've still got Willy round our necks, and I tell him he can wear my bobbed hat if he goes for the bog-rolls and Arfer fetches him another, and he goes home for them.

And Arfer and me went up all the back alleys so he won't know which way we've gone, and then there's us two on the coach and ten minutes later we're still there, 'cause the big man's late himself. And we see Willy coming up the pavement, yelling to the driver half a mile off not to go without him, but our bloke gets here first and won't let Willy on and tells him to scarper.

And he told them there would be a nosh-up after the match, and they must stick together if they did not want to be left behind in Parkeston. And there was likely to be some rough stuff on the stands, Parkeston being docks and that, and if anybody did start suffink, they was to bundle in together.

A black night, with a lot of stars that did not seem to achieve much in the way of illumination: they sang along the Colchester by-pass—*Hi, hi, Cafoozalem, the harlot of Jerusalem* and *Star of the Evening, shining on the shit-house door.*

They pulled up somewhere, and the bleeding driver did not know where the ground was, he'd have to ask. They must be somewhere near the docks, because there were cranes, and sea-gulls piss-hooking about, and a smell like yesterday's fish-heads. Then there were these bloody nits going past with banners and signs that no bugger could read anyway on a night like this, and they had rucksacks and guitars and blanket-rolls and that.

The Finsbury mob had got out for a slash and somebody like started cat-calling, and the word went round that this lot called themselves *Peace for Plenty*, nut-cases route-marching to the boat so they could go and shout ban the bleeding bomb in Munich or somewhere. Somebody remembered the pebbles in his pocket, and they started giving the silly buggers *Peace and Plenty*. Nobody knew where the fuzz came from, and that lot didn't care whether it was commies or innocent football supporters they was sailing into.

All that Arfer knew afterwards was that Geoff was alive and kicking when they all got nicked. Well, it wasn't a proper nick, just a waiting-room or suffink on the station, that the Bill had taken over. But Geoff was dead with the base of his skull cracked when they carried him out again on a stretcher.

Two deaths—not likely to be connected in men's minds for a long time. Kenworthy had not heard of either of them when he presented himself to the guard at Reception, the Duchy of Axholme, on the Monday morning. Because neither was important enough for inclusion in any news bulletin he had heard. And he had made no contact with Forrester or Bransby-Lowndes because he did not want to be side-tracked. Whippletree—Pascoe—Mather—Iliffe: that was the order of the day. Then he might think of reporting back to the Faculty.

It was the same guard that Kenworthy had met at the conference, a man that he knew he ought to have recognized. He made the effort now to place the cropped white hair, to ignore the moderate beer-drinker's paunch, to slim the man down. A natural respector of persons, this one, but by no means a crawler. It made his day to see Kenworthy again.

And then Kenworthy knew him: Winchmore Hill, in the 1950's: a 1950's murder—no mystery, no forensic ingenuity, no chase. It was one of those family inevitables that one met rather less often in this nuance of middle-class. The only real concern was to get it all docketed at once, so that it could all be put away and the next call answered: everything said that everyone needed to say, and all the exhibits logged and labelled.

And the constable on door-duty had stretched a point—used his bloody silly initiative—to let the married daughter of the house go into the undusted sitting-room to get her cigarettes from the mantelpiece. Cigarettes that were needed for logging and labelling. On a Kenworthy case! Kenworthy the winnowing fan—in those days. Constable 496 Peters had quaked. Kenworthy said nothing, did not report him to his division, let him get away with being a good-natured, bumbling fool. Made a friend for life.

'I want to see Mr P.P. Whippletree. He isn't expecting me.'

'I'll see what I can do, Mr Kenworthy.'

'So when you'd served your time, you still couldn't stay out of uniform?'

'You're lucky to catch me still here, Mr Kenworthy. I'm moving to Natsecure.'

'Natsecure?'

'A good lot to be with, Mr Kenworthy. Best move I could make.'

'Really?'

'Know where you stand on hours. No bullshit beyond what any man can see the need for. More than one of your old pals in top office. Surprised you haven't given it a thought, sir.'

'What, me? I've got a garden that needs me. Who's the top lot, then?'

Bragg, Kershaw, Barraclough, Tyrrell—

'Mr Cawthorne.'

Kenworthy did not let it hit him—did not let it be seen to hit him.

'I know he was always said to be a hard man, Mr Kenworthy. But I always had a square deal by him. You know where you stand with Mr Cawthorne.'

Mr Cawthorne: Kenworthy had looked for him at Egham as soon as he had seen the others there. Forrester had said he was high up in Natsecure. Cawthorne was a name that by telepathic agreement was never mentioned in the Kenworthy household: because his blood pressure was not all that it used to be, and Elspeth deserved not to have to hear it all again. Even Forrester, thinking—as he must now and then—about Kenworthy's departure from the Yard—would have been circumspect about bringing Cawthorne's name up.

'See if you can raise Mr Whippletree for me, please, Peters.'

Whippletree kept him waiting, was not the bouncing iconoclast that he had found oddly attractive at the conference. Whippletree looked as if he was under the sort of hangover that couldn't stand the delay much longer of a shot of Scotch. Except that for various reasons, Kenworthy did not believe it was a hangover. There was a sleepless night behind Whippletree: a lack of appetite—and not only for food. Whippletree was finding it hard to put his mind to the very simple proposition that Kenworthy was making to him.

Nor did all the confidential reports on the man seem all that credible. Flaunting unsuitable dress? Whippletree was Millbank Man down to the final tightening of his tie: except that his sagging shoulders were doing nothing for a suit of which Bransby-Lowndes would not have been ashamed. A practical joker? He did not look as if he could ever have the energy to try.

'I'll tell you what it is. I must confess I rather enjoyed myself at your little civil-commotion get-together. And I could do with any odd guineas that drop into my palm. So really I'm here to ask, if you're ever doing anything like it again—it's a subject on which I'm not without ideas, though I say it myself. I don't just mean lobbing out the *Leberwurst* in the German backwoods.'

The approach direct. He was perfectly entitled—and qualified—to try for ground-floor entry. But Whippletree received it glassily. Kenworthy wondered if he had taken it all in.

'You see, I have the time. I'm not without relevant experience. I have the taste for it—'

Whippletree stirred himself, dutifully, lethargically.

'I'm afraid, you know, that business at Egham—it was one off. Not what we're really in business for, in the Duchy. It was just something that arose out of one of our reports. I've no reason to think we shall be mounting anything like it again.'

'I see.'

And was the interview now deemed concluded? Kenworthy carried on with simplistic brightness.

'I thought I'd ask. No harm in trying.'

'Sorry I can't do anything for you. I was only conference bursar. Dogsbody: the chap who forgot to lay the special diet on for the vegans.'

A hint of the return to the old Whippletree? It was certainly not followed up.

'Maybe I'd better have a word with someone higher up in the hierarchy. Who was the young lady that I also met at Egham? I think you introduced her as your boss.'

Whippletree looked at him as if slow-wittedly.

'Miss Pascoe, was it?'

'Miss Pascoe won't be in this morning.'

Said in the tone of a man hoping that that would end the matter.

'And I can't say when she will be.'

'Not ill, I hope?'

'Personal matters.'

It would not have been surprising if Whippletree had risen at that point to end the dialogue. But he remained seated for a few more listless seconds. Kenworthy bulldozed on.

'Well, look, let's not pretend. I don't come into things with my eyes closed. I never have led that kind of life. Anyone who knows where to lay hands on a Whitaker can get hold of your set-up. It's obviously your Mr Mather I ought to ask to see.'

'Percival Mather is dead.'

'I'm sorry. I didn't know that.'

'Friday night, suddenly.'

And having said it, Whippletree seemed in some measure relieved.

'So I'm afraid the helm is swinging about a bit this morning. I'm sorry if I seem unhelpful. But even in the long run, I don't see much chance that you'll be offered anything here. Your better hope would be to approach MoD direct.'

'Thank you. Perhaps I'll do that.'

As he went out, he spoke only briefly to ex-PC Peters, who was trying to bracket somebody on the switchboard.

'I'm still on the lookout for a chance to buy you a pint.'

Left to himself Forrester might have lapsed into that crudity that is not uncommon in men who believe themselves inured to sudden death. In Bransby-Lowndes's presence, he had to do lip-service to the decencies.

'It seems that Judith Pascoe—the last person on earth of whom anyone expected it—took her boss home after a West End scoff for a Civil Service massage session. And, putting it bluntly, he had a coronary on the job. A nasty experience for a sheltered young lady.'

'That explains why I was unable to get an appointment with her this morning.'

'She's taken a few days' leave to get over it. The local police know her whereabouts, though I see no reason why they should need them. His doctor had seen him within the last fortnight to renew prescriptions. He says this could have happened any minute of the last fifteen years. Even at that, the coroner asked for a post mortem, to be on the safe side. That was done late on Saturday and showed the expected cardiac infarct. There won't be an inquest. The girl was shattered. Went right to pieces.'

Kenworthy tried to conjure up a working memory from their encounter at the conference. A photographic image was elusive, but he remembered finding her exceptionally agreeable. And—superficially, at any rate—he would not have predicted moral laxity. But what was moral laxity? He knew that something had happened in the 'sixties—and that a lot of things had stayed as they always had been.

'Was she making a habit of sleeping with him?'

'It seems not. But it's not been gone into all that deeply. Her first reaction was to deny anything untoward—in the teeth of all the evidence. She seemed quite unreasonably determined to defend her honour, up to the waist in the last ditch.'

'In the teeth of what evidence?' Kenworthy asked, perhaps a shade more sharply than he had wanted to sound. Forrester glanced at Bransby-Lowndes as if for permission to proceed.

'Oh, tell him, Forrester. You know you're dying to get down to detail.'

'He was wearing only his pyjama top. Sperm drying on the sheet, a stain roughly the shape of the Isle of Wight.'

'There's no need to be so bloody picturesque,' Bransby-Lowndes said.

'Your geographical associations are not evidence,' Kenworthy said. 'And you say she tried to deny it?'

'Virtual collapse of her faculties. Talked arrant nonsense.'

'And she's gone away to rest?'

'We can put a finger on her. I don't see that it should be necessary. A very unhappy business altogether.'

'Had Mather family?'

'A wife older than himself—in her late sixties, diabetic. Two grown-up children, now rallying round. The widow thought he'd gone out of town on an inter-departmental working party.'

'I can see why people are upset.'

Including Whippletree.

Bransby-Lowndes had a paper in his hand, and had been waiting to hand it to Forrester as soon as they had disposed of the main business.

'Another of these flimsies—the first you'll have seen, Kenworthy. Similar theme and variations to what we've had before: Friday night at Harwich. Small disturbance, but the police task force—not *called* an SPG—seems to have been out of all proportion to the punch-up. It was just a small band of one-offers, pilgrims, not even affiliated to CND. They'd walked from Birmingham to Parkeston Quay, complaints from outraged householders wherever they dossed down, and they intended crossing Holland and Germany on foot to get to some rally. But there was also a minor league football match and a bunch of hoodlums who just look as if they might have been organized. They got mixed up in it somehow, which loosed off the hounds. Only this time a London kid got himself killed, apparently in custody. Reports from that point on are what they call confused. This is going to be nasty for somebody. Let's hope we don't have to do more than read the carbons.'

'You say you've had a lot of these? Why are you getting them? What are the common features?'

'The Duchy just made us think that perhaps soccer cowboys were worth a second look. The fixture is often quite an obscure one. It's often a small band of hooligans, who could — just *could* — have been put up to it. Sometimes, not always, there's a hairy demonstration in the offing. And sometimes there's a police presence waiting in the wings that's big enough for some to call it provocative.'

'You have all this on the file?'

'I don't know what else we can do with it, until something crystallizes out.'

'Like this poor kid on Friday?'

'I can see this one going on for months: parental appeals against coroners' verdicts.'

'I'll run my eye down that file while I'm here.'

Judith Pascoe took an afternoon walk on the fen. The salt of an up-tide breeze dried her lips. Men and women were few and far between in the flat fields under the great hemisphere of sky.

It had recalled to her — and she was masochist enough to have meant that it should — the other decision that she had once come here to make. Then there had been, let her be honest, a tinge of self-satisfied priggishness about the outcome. What the hell? If she was a prig, she was a prig. She had had to force that decision out of herself, or flounder at the crucial stage of her M. Litt. thesis. She would damned well have that on her hands at a time like this.

She had let a man go, because — oh, this was *de facto* God's honest truth — because it would have wrecked too many other lives if she hadn't. She could have lived with him. She was not sure in that indulgent moment how she was going to live without him. But she could not have lived with *that*—the mess of truly deserved unforgiveness ineradicable behind her.

So she had borrowed the key to the man's retreat—he was the don who was supervising her research—and he had known she was coming out here to think it all out. It was the first time she had slept here without him. And once she came to a conclusion, there would be no going back on that.

It had resolved itself very civilly. So civilly that she had been able to ring him up that Sunday morning in Highgate. Could she borrow the cottage for a day or two? She knew he would not come out and disturb her, would not want to know why.

She was fond of the fens. You either were, or they got you down. It wasn't nature—the way the land had been drained and harnessed. The landscape itself was an artefact—monotous, geometrical, aggressively unexotic. It was a victory of man over environment—but you had the feeling that the environment was only waiting for its chance: a high wind, a spring tide, frost in the sea-wall.

It was conducive to making up minds. But this time the process was no trouble. It turned out that even the memories of last time weren't triggers of agony; only foolishness.

Well, first she had to eat sensibly, sleep till she needed no more sleep, get reasonable exercise: *in corpore sano*. As for *mens sana*: she had a mad memory to put behind her—though it was remarkable how it had seemed to recede of its own accord as the train cast its dye-line across the black fields round Ely.

It had been madness, the scene that she had come back to in Highgate—a Monty Python abnegation of reality, a Spike Milligan montage, a Pieter Breughel *Dulle Griet*. Was it to be wondered at that the police had reached the conclusions they had? But it was infuriating to the point at which something had surely had to snap. She had been about as articulate with the CID as Percy Mather wrestling with one of his special inadequacies.

Percy Mather: a melancholy memory. That was the word he had used himself about the Duchy. She knew now that he had been murdered. He had been murdered because, for all his stutterings, old Percy had not been as inadequate as all that. He had talked to her about danger: had used that word, too. He had seen danger in a ploy that she did not know that Peter Paul had on, a ploy about Public Opinion Polls.

Did men do murder for the sake of Public Opinion Polls? Obviously, it was political high explosive, setting out to discredit them. It could tumble a politician, perhaps. A party might lose marginal credence. Even a tabloid might be made to writhe a bit.

But murder?

No; but there were other things going on at the Duchy of Axholme — things that she was pretty certain Peter Paul knew about. And how much had Percy known? What else had he been planning to tell her?

Why did her mind keep coming back to Peter Paul Whippletree? Why did it seem so important to her all of a sudden to convince Peter Paul that she had not slept with Percy? There was nothing between her and Whippletree, beyond the banter of an office relationship. Why did she keep coming back to him as a potential ally?

Because she needed an ally. The police would only laugh at her, as they must have been laughing behind their hands last Friday. She rejected the police — if only because she knew she had not got it in her to convince them.

But Kenworthy would listen. Something about Kenworthy had intrigued her at the conference. Everybody else who had talked at Egham had been aching for trouble, wanting it to start, wanting to move in and fulfil themselves, arming themselves with riot-shields for fighting in the streets. Kenworthy had so obviously hated the mindlessness of it all. She had gone back from Egham to Millbank to dig up something about him from files to which Iliffe of Security had access. She could use the Duchy prerogative to get hold of his ex-directory home number.

She saw the action ahead as cool, immutable, once she had grasped it in outline. She had come to the Fens to reach such a decision, had been prepared for it to take her three days to find it.

Now she slipped Ian MacIntyre's copy of Elliott's *Runes* back on its shelf and decided that one night of salt air would suffice.

CHAPTER 7

There was an unevenness about the carbons that reported violence to the Faculty. Some police forces were selective, some submitted every street-corner punch-up. Others only remembered at intervals to send anything at all. Kenworthy was under no illusion about the closing decades of the twentieth century: there was no more urban violence now than one read of in Arthur Morrison's tales of Victorian poverty. But what Morrison's slums had not suffered was organization, co-ordination, mobility. There was an intelligence service at work now. Trouble-makers could be shipped into spots where uproar was pending—or where it was about to be provoked.

He found notes of three cases with suggestively common features. In Cambridge last autumn, a small, nicely mannered band of young children, their law-abiding parents, the Chairman of their Parish Council, their vicar and a spokesman for their free churches had come one afternoon to parade outside the County Offices, protesting with posters against the closure of their village school. Television crews were there by appointment; children from the top class spoke prepared little speeches into the microphone: well disciplined sentimental symbols. Two panda cars, parked at a discreet distance, were there to facilitate the demonstration, not to suppress it.

But this was counting without a gang of yobbos, mid-adolescents, who happened along a side-street as if they'd sniffed trouble by instinct. Education Committee members arrived, were canvassed, a petition was handed over by a well-brought-up nine-year old. Then, since Guy Fawkes' Day was approaching, someone threw a firework. A group tried to overturn a councillor's car.

It was a mild outbreak, leading to three arrests, sentences of community service — and the escape of many of the layabouts, who were able to retreat in several directions. It seemed they were football spectators from the Royston area, whiling away mischievous hours before an evening match. The few who were caught were sullen, uncooperative, truculently anti-police, appeared too stupid to know who had organized their outing.

The second case had been in Bradford in depth of winter. A cruising patrol had performed a two-car pincer movement on a pub forecourt brawl between natives and Asiatics, only to have their attention distracted by a gang of about twenty who had started fighting among themselves in a further corner of the poorly lit, snow-slushy square. They were pursued. They dispersed. And there were no satisfactory answers about how and why this bunch came to be where they were: or who had signalled them to start their affray at the tactical moment best calculated to impede the police.

Then, in March, along the perimeter of a small-components factory on Humberside, police had moved in to disperse secondary pickets who were obstructing the highway in a strength ludicrously disproportionate to the small work-force involved. Many of those picked up had no Trade Union affiliations. Some were Technical College students who claimed to be present only as spectators of a social phenomenon. In addition, the police had charged a number of seventeen- and eighteen-year-olds with carrying knuckle-dusters and sand-filled socks. Many of these youngsters were unemployed — some unemployable, in the low intelligence bracket. No one revealed who had convened them and got them to the factory gates. Did many of them neither know nor care?

Were they, like the Cambridge mob, *too stupid to know?* Hoodlums of low mentality, marshalled on a small scale, on a narrowly local basis? Were these only the early stages? Kenworthy raked the files for evidence that any of these groups had been used more than once; and that was not apparent. So perhaps it had not passed the stage of recruitment and preliminary try-out. They would need some sort of primitive training; elementary battle tactics; route discipline; systematic armament.

If Bransby-Lowndes's fears were grounded, some of these squads of morons could be sent in next time a riot squad had its hands full. They would add to the confusion, if nothing worse, create diversions. A few kids would get hurt by those who were supposed to be maintaining the Queen's Peace. It had happened before. It would happen again. It was going to grow. It was being put together by someone who knew why he wanted it to happen.

And yet in certain public places, it paid to play such notions down. The poor old Home Secretary at Question Time could create community panic with a few careless syllables. But out on the ground there had to be men who looked at hideous fantasies and asked themselves, what if this were fact? Kenworthy had not expected to find himself out on the ground again.

Forrester was yearning to be out on the ground. He was a man who had got where he was largely by intuitive management of his own reputation. And not just reputation: Forrester *was* tough. His promotions had been into and out of the vintage Flying Squad. He was unyielding, demanding, preferred to scoff at the thought of ever being considered subtle. His impatience had kept his sergeants nimble. He was scathing of regulations and personalities that threatened to delay him.

And yet he had always stayed out of trouble in areas where trouble was endemic. He had been up before A 10 — who hadn't, for Christ's sake? And he'd always come out grinning. His contempt for rules was a legend: yet could anyone ever prove an infringement? Forrester had always managed his life on two fronts without apparent effort. You didn't become Chief Investigating Officer at Cabinet disposal if you were tabbed as a risk.

But when it came to an excursion into the field to talk to the Kings — Geoff's family — he ignored the house-rules. He knew that Bransby-Lowndes would never give him clearance for it, still less ungum the channels to let Kenworthy in. He knew that he'd be looked upon as a saboteur by the local station, who'd be struggling to get something going with the Kings. There would be pressmen to be decoyed. But he had to go. There were questions that he had to ask, to which he would be lucky to get answers. He could not stand the thought that someone else might fail where he had not even chanced his arm.

The Kings lived in a block of pre-war Buildings between Hackney and Stoke Newington. GLC policy had been for this barrack to devolve into the homeland of a sub-tribe, among whom the Kings did not stand out. Some said it was wrong to assemble a depressed community in one place with a common outlook. But if you didn't, decent people might get them as neighbours. Whatever you decided, it went sour.

Albert King, 52, was described in some documents as an electrician's mate. No one remembered what stage in his past endeavours that referred to. King was uncompromisingly opposed to everything and everyone outside his own outlook. He did not merely suspect goodwill: he knew no particular reason to admit of its existence. He was vague about the mechanics of society, though he believed that there was an inner cartel concerned only with its own interests. If pressed for details—if in a mood to converse at all—he might have said that brewers and chain-bookmakers were somewhere near the heart of the machine. And the Stock Exchange.

King would never turn to the police over any wrong done to him. He would not cooperate with the Bill in any circumstances. If they ever appeared to be on his side, that was double reason to distrust them. The 'murder' of his son in a railway waiting-room on Parkeston Quay had in a way been a godsend. It confirmed all he had ever believed. He even refused any communication from the young, unpaid, community-mission solicitor who was trying to get the matter into his hands. Later, when unique opportunities had been missed, when memories were befogged and appeals were out of time, Albert King might have a brainstorm and demand action.

There would be no question of admitting Forrester to his home. He wouldn't even open the door to him, the intelligence system of the Buildings having somehow got the message through the walls that Forrester was on his way up. But Forrester had developed arcane talents. He could make a lot of frightening noise with his shoulder at a door.

This one was opened to him now as the only defence against a battery that must be destructive. Without appearing to move, Forrester's foot slipped forward to a spot from which there was no hope of ever shifting it.

'What do you bleeding want?'

King did not know Forrester, but did not need to be told how he earned his living.

'To come in.'

And Forrester was in, looking round with insulting distaste. There was evidence on the table that the Kings sometimes ate: a plate with crumbs of pork pie crust clinging to a generous smear of sauce: not a family meal. The Kings did not have meals or meal-times according to a pattern. The Old Woman had notions: she tried to lay the law down sometimes, had once tried to get a habit of Sunday dinner going. But how can you serve Sunday dinner when people don't come in for it? There was food in the cupboard, as often as not. Sometimes someone would open a tin. Sometimes they would have to fight the Old Woman for it — and lose. Sometimes a purse would be opened, and chips would be gone out for: sometimes a purse would be rifled for the same purpose. Sometimes the pilfering had to be from outside sources.

Forrester took them all in. Albert King, short-limbed, breathing badly, stood on his rights.

'You ain't got—'

'I'm here. That's what matters.'

The Old Woman, five years younger than her husband, had in early middle age achieved the raddled blonde look by means of cheap dyes and rinses. She seemed to want to cling to the memory of the style, though every last shred of colour had now retreated into a perfunctorily combed grey. Her hormone-starved wrinkles were a hopeless basis for the startling contrast of her cosmetics: when she put on cheap rouge, she played for the full effect. For all their squalor, she was a woman who believed in cosmetics; they had become part of her. She was smoking a cigarette which never left her lips. She blew occasionally to detach ash.

Forrester did not know her, but he knew her type. On no issue would she ever deign to agree with her husband or offspring. She ran her matriarchal nest through the fear of her tongue. But faced with an outsider, her loyalty to her family was ferocious.

'What I want to know, is when can we bury our Geoff?'

Being deprived, up to now, of a funeral, was something worth latching on to.

Arfer was reading a coverless paperback — a Western — which he was holding rolled into a kind of loose cylinder. He sniggered every now and then over the desperado dialogue. He did not acknowledge that Forrester was in the room.

'I want you to tell me, laddie, in your own words, precisely what happened at Parkeston.'

'Oh no he don't. He tells nobody nothing but what he told that bloody coroner.'

'If he won't tell me here, he can come round the nick.'

'So you can top him too? No, mate. He don't open his mouth, don't walk a yard, without my solicitor's with him.'

To achieve that, Albert might even admit the young nit from the community mission. The only solicitors he had ever had to do with were legal aid briefs, who had never stood much of a chance.

Forrester moved his position so that he could look at the fourth member of the family. The room smelled of steam, stale tobacco, chips and belched beer. Willy was at a corner of the table idly bombing an old newspaper with a ballpoint. A pouting, snivelling boy, he did not look as if he would ever harden off, as his brothers had, to absorb the bludgeonings that were coming to him. Willy was soft-centred. Perhaps it was because of his age and position in the family. Maybe his head had been smacked once too often by one too many. Forrester knew then where to get ingress into the darker shadows of the Kings. It would mean hanging about a bit. Willy had to be seen and talked to outside the home.

One heard stories, of course, about Sir Henry and his snuff-boxes, but the Permanent Secretary's impact on the Duchy was so slight that those in the middle reaches, like Whippletree, had to perform an act of faith to believe at all in his existence. Or, at least, they might have believed in it had they cared whether he existed or not. On the Tuesday morning following Percy's death, Whippletree was sent for by the top office.

Sir Henry did not even mention Restoration silver. Whippletree was relieved. He had looked up a few references, to arm himself with courteous frivolities in case gaps in the dialogue had to be weathered.

But Sir Henry was in no easy frame of mind. It was rumoured that one of the Deputy Secretaries— presumably Killer Burton—occasionally bullied him, when his authority, his name or a token of his presence was needed to back up some administrative shit's trick that was being cooked up by the middle management. It followed that Sir Henry's rare pronouncements were often unpopular ones, and it was reported by those few who had ever heard one that his discomfort was as great as that of the recipient.

It was the Tuesday morning—too early, perhaps by months, for anything to have been decided about a replacement for old Percy. It was the second day of Judith Pascoe's absence. Bolger, Asst Sec. of IV (Parliamentary) had been given a watching brief over III (Populace). He was giving no trouble: had merely inquired if everyone had enough to do, and told them to get on with it. Then came half an hour's notice to Whippletree to present himself upstairs.

'Ah! Whippletree. We have met, I think. Your father

was the 16th/12th?'

'My uncle, sir. My father was the Duke of Teesdale's Own.'

'Quite so. My error. But you were at St Martin's?'

Whippletree's early warning systems went on immediate alert. School mattered so much to these imbeciles. And by comparison with what was thought of him at St Martin's he had been canonized by the Civil Service Commissioners.

'Just been glancing through this paper of yours on Opinion Polls.'

So they'd been at Percy's files already.

'Sterling job. Sterling job. Only thing is, we have to watch trends, you know. It can hardly go forward in the form that it is.'

Yes: Sir Henry had had his orders from Killer.

'Who actually authorized this report, Whippletree? Who set, as it were, the wheels, as it were, in motion?'

'Mr Mather did know about it, sir.'

There was something poetically just in being able, for once, to shelter behind Percy. It was touching to be able to tell the approximate truth about the dead. It was emphatically against Duchy policy for anyone in Whippletree's grade to initiate a Study without hard-won ratification from above.

'Sterling job. Though you were lucky, of course, to get hold of a man who passed on such compromising papers.'

Luck? Half an hour in a pub with a man who was as cheesed-off with his circumstances as Whippletree was.

'I mean. Quite damning, this business of being told what percentages to aim at before asking your questions. Got to be careful it doesn't reflect on others. There are honest pollsters.'

'Yes, Sir Henry. Most of them. I have only impugned two. I thought I had made that carefully clear.'

'Loss of public confidence, you know. People don't like

voting for certain losers.'

That was the object of the exercise, of course—but it seemed pointless going over that for Sir Henry. He wouldn't have listened very closely to what Killer had come griping to him about.

'Don't want to look like a pack of snoopers, you know. Better get this looked over by someone with his finger on the pulse. All your supporting papers—let Burton run his eye over them. Good man, Burton. Has an eye for snags.'

And could be relied on to kill this one as dead as a crow under a tractor.

'Yes, sir.'

'Give yourself a rest from it till Burton's had a word with you. Got something else to be getting on with, I feel sure.'

'Plenty, sir.'

Including the Boxing Day Bumper Square. It was the first time they had asked him to tackle an outsize. It would take a good week of office time.

'My regards to your father, Whippletree. And your uncle.'

'Both dead, sir.'

CHAPTER 8

Once the decision was made, Judith Pascoe felt as if the life about her had taken on a different pace. The fenland landscape had not changed, but the hedges seemed alive now, the trees were breathing, the cottage walls, roofs and chimneys were quickened with people's lives. She was sorry now to be leaving this countryside; she had seen so little of it this time. She knew, of course, that difficulties, complications, lay ahead.

She had no intention of looking in at the office until she

returned officially tomorrow. And she hated the thought of ever going back to live in that flat. She tried to dismiss all pictures of that from her mind. And she tried to get through on the phone to Peter Paul, the only personality within the Duchy with whom she felt she could bear to have contact. She rang him from a village call-box somewhere south of Cambridge.

But he did not answer on his extension. She asked for one of the clerical officers, but could not locate him through her, either. But the same clerk was able to get her Kenworthy's ex-directory number.

Then she had to organize change to get to ring Kenworthy. When she heard his voice, it struck her how little she knew of the man. Wouldn't he fall in line with the rest of them, after he had heard her story?

She would not commit herself to details on the phone. He did not seem to expect her to. There were serious matters, she told him, on which she would like his opinion. She hoped she was not wasting his time. He replied with genial courtesy, a hint of friendliness, subdued but promising. What she had said about him at the conference: common sense and goodwill. He would be delighted to put himself at her disposal. His voice seemed to make light in advance of impossibilities.

Would she have time en route to find a suburban hairdresser with a cancellation in which she could get a shampoo and set? She drove in an unnecessarily wide loop to avoid the temptation to call in at Highgate.

The Kenworthys received her with a warmth that would not have come amiss towards a member of their family. Mrs Kenworthy was a comfortable, domesticated woman, apparently accustomed to having problems dropped at her fireside. She also gave the impression of seeing round a few corners on her own account; of seeing more in Judith Pacoe than would meet most people's eyes; and of rather liking what she saw.

Kenworthy was doing something involving secateurs and twine in their small garden. He came indoors in a massively loose pullover that made him look like a safely tame bear, throwing a hat like Paddington's on to a kitchen chair. Not until butter was melting into toasted tea-cakes did he slant an eyebrow to invite her to start talking business. It was only then that the taste for telling it became nasty in her mouth again.

'On Saturday night, my boss took me out to dinner.'

The Kenworthys would know that. Only now did the full weight hit her of how much they must know.

'Your former colleagues, the police, have formed their own idea as to why he should do that. May I ask you to keep an open mind about it? I can't stop you from drawing your own conclusions when I've finished.'

Kenworthy conveyed that he was entirely in her hands. Elspeth Kenworthy looked on wholly sympathetically.

'He did it, I think, partly because he wanted my company — and also because there were things about our work that he wanted to tell me. I am a newcomer to the Duchy and his branch. I am just finding my feet — and I like to think he was just coming to think he could trust me.'

She was beginning to look on the Kenworthys as the same class of people as her own parents. There was a similar suggestion of domestic give and take, out of which had grown a sort of telepathic common front.

'What he wanted to pass on to me may not be all that important.'

'I think it well may,' Kenworthy said.

'It was routine office stuff. He did use the word 'dangerous' — but in Civil Service terms that only means potentially embarrassing. Percy Mather was a man who suffered from pathological diffidence — until he became used to a particular person's company. That was how he came to the Duchy in the first instance. You know something, I take it, of the zany history of the department?'

'I think we can take that as read.'

'This was concerned with a man called Whippletree. You met him briefly at Egham.'

'I remember. And before you go on, I have seen career-biographical notes.'

'Yes, well, a lot of people think they know a lot about him. Peter Paul may be his own worst enemy, but he has outside enemies too. But don't let me stray from the main line. Peter Paul is a loner. He has no respect for the establishment. And his experience in the Duchy has done nothing to give him any. He keeps himself happy by composing highly disciplined crosswords — and also from time to time by using the machinery of the Duchy to go in depth into things that it amuses him to go into. One of the things he has put his finger on recently has been a transparent attempt by certain Opinion Polls to juggle figures in advance of by-elections. Percy Mather was impressed by his outline report and obviously, if and when the news breaks, it's going to have the makings of a minor sensation. Mr Mather wanted me to know that he was going to back that report. And he hoped that I'd see my way to doing so too. That gives you the colour of the man: no compulsion, no appeal to arbitrary loyalty, no internal blackmail. An honest hope.'

'And you will be backing it?'

'I don't know. I haven't seen the report yet. But that isn't the point. I have the feeling, and it's a strong one, that there were other things that Percy wanted to tell me — if the evening had not worked out the way that it did. The Duchy is a weird place, and there are some weird things going on in it.'

'Like your conference on civil unrest.'

'My role at Egham was purely administrative: to see that the wheels turned, that projectionists were booked, that films had arrived, and so on. I cannot tell you much more about it than that — except that I saw some things that I disliked very much indeed. But I am getting away from the main story again.'

'Sorry,' Kenworthy said, and nothing could have sounded more genuine.

'When we got up from the meal, I noticed that Percy wasn't looking well. I mean, he was little more than a stranger to me, and for all I know, he may have looked unwell most of the time. The things he had wanted to talk about had put him under additional strain, and when we got up to go, I noticed that he seemed to be swaying on his feet, as if he were on the verge of a faint. But he insisted on taking me home in a taxi. It was when we came to get out that I thought he looked very ill indeed. He didn't deny he felt ill, agreed to come in, and asked if I had any spirits, preferably brandy, in the house.

'I took him in and I got him upstairs — and by now he needed physical help. He told me he had a bad heart and there were drugs in a phial in his waistcoat pocket that I helped him to get at. But the stuff did him no good. I got him into an armchair, and he said he really did think I ought to try to get him a doctor. I went to my phone, and it was dead. I said I would go out and phone from a box — or go round to the surgery. It isn't more than five minutes' walk away.'

There were red flush-spots over her cheek-bones now. This stage of her story had cost emotional exertion.

'The kiosk in Spaniards Road had been vandalized. I had some difficulty in making myself heard at the surgery — it was after ten — and even more difficulty in getting past a doctor's wife who was playing the defensive spouse. I suppose it was quite twenty minutes before I got back to the flat.'

And there she had met a sight far removed from the cosiness of the Kenworthys' sitting-room, in which very little was new, and everything must have its associations.

'By then, Percy Mather was dead. His clothes had been taken off him and folded tidily over one of my chairs. He had been put in my bed, which was in suggestive disarray. He was wearing only a pyjama jacket. His pyjama trousers—or, shall we say, somebody's pyjama trousers, a pair I had certainly never seen before—had been thrown over the foot of my bed. And there was other misleading evidence of the kind that the public used to find offensive.'

'I know.'

'I can assure you that Mr Mather brought nothing with him to my flat—no case, no package of any description. I told all this to several levels of policeman. I was not hysterical, and I do not think my statements varied in any significant detail. They evidently thought I was out of my mind, trying to claim black was white, hoping to cling to my moral virtue in face of incontrovertible evidence. When I maintained the same story, even after the preliminary medical reports, I think they wrote me off as a witness. I went away for a couple of days to think things into perspective. And here I am—'

She looked at Kenworthy, waiting for his reaction. It was not immediate.

'Well?' she asked him.

'Well what?'

'Do you believe me?'

He looked surprised.

'You have just told us what happened.'

'I suppose I must have begun to doubt my own plain experience.'

'I don't see why you should.'

He seemed to accept it all with a childlike simplicity.

'There is nothing in what you have described that could not have been staged by someone who knew precisely how he wanted things to look. Of course, there are details of

execution that require explanation. I have no doubt that
they can all be explained.'

Kenworthy's wife went to put fresh water into the
teapot.

'There are just one or two questions—'

'There are bound to be.'

He was now looking suitably serious, as if apologizing in
advance for what had to be asked.

'This man Whippletree—you cannot have known him
long?'

'A few weeks. He is one of my working team.'

'I wonder if you have seen his personal file—or been
warned what is in it?'

'You mean tales that are told about him? A disgusting
thing he's supposed to have done at his first Ministry,
when there was an Iron Curtain visit? I do assure you, Mr
Kenworthy, that *canard* must be unfounded. He is a most
fastidious young man.'

'But it's true to say, isn't it, that he has changed in some
ways from the young rebel he once was? I spoke to him
yesterday morning, and he seemed to me the very soul of
a public servant. He is, for example, a sartorial model.'

'Oh, that? Well, yes—he admits he has changed. He
says that that's something that came to him quite late in
life—he talks like that, you'd think he was in his
seventies—He says life would have been a lot easier for
him if only he'd learned one lesson earlier on: that if you
want to be a nonconformist in things that matter, it pays
to conform in things that don't. It saves misunder-
standings that you can do without.'

Both the Kenworthys laughed, but Kenworthy did not
keep it up long.

'That's all very well. But let's talk for a moment about
some of the big things. It all amounts, doesn't it, to
throwing pepper into the eyes of the establishment
whenever he can?'

'And oh, how I envy him his nerve!'

Did she catch the Kenworthys exchanging a quick glance?

'I dare say. I'm sure he's a very amusing character to have around any office.'

'All right. And I'll admit, there are some quarters in which we could do with a little amusement. But there's more to him than that.'

Then she laughed at herself, but not mirthfully. She knew that she was bearing witness to a Peter Paul Whippletree that she had not fully admitted to herself.

'I don't see that he really enters into this very closely,' she said, knowing how lame that was.

'No? Yet he was the one Mather wanted to talk to you about, wasn't he?'

'For all I know, Mr Mather may have said all he wanted to say about him. In any case, he was wholly on his side. Let me put it in Whippletree's own words—'

She hated to go through the salutary motions of having another little laugh at herself.

'You'll think we must have found time in office hours to say a good deal to each other. We'd taken to having morning coffee together, other engagements permitting. And Peter Paul is a breathless talker who doesn't like not being understood. He put it in his own words to me, his reason for not caring for the established order. He doesn't like physical pain, ball games bore him, and he doesn't care for *espirit de corps* unless he has himself chosen the *corps*.'

'A full house.'

'He went to one of those public schools where young boys are no longer officially allowed to beat younger ones. So they do it unofficially—of which the housemasters are well aware. On his first night at St Martin's, he was viciously caned for having such a stupid name as Whippletree. This was an initiation ceremony, and

therefore it was hallowed as a tradition. It was carried out
by those boys who had missed appointment as house-
prefects that year. Much earlier in his life, his father,
teaching him to play cricket on a beach, had cracked him
across the shin with a child's iron spade. And at his prep
school a games coach, seeing his nervousness, had tried to
cure it by fielding him close to the bat, which got him a
fractured patella.'

'And he'd never grown out of all this?'

She came back at him with a burst of sudden anger.

'It had left him impatient with morons,' she said.

Elspeth came to her rescue.

'I could tell you a story about Simon. More than one.'

But Kenworthy was into something. He did not desist.

'I am sorry, Miss Pascoe. But you must allow me a few
more tactless questions. I do not guarantee that you will
like me for asking them.'

She took control of herself, invited him not to spare
her.

'Did Whippletree know that Mather was taking you out
to dinner?'

'He did.'

'And how did he react to that?'

'With heavy humour.'

She thought back to some of the things he had said: old
Percy's erogenous zones; de-erection; impregnating a
typing-pool. She hoped Kenworthy was not going to press
for the actual jokes.

'He was jealous, in fact?'

She blushed.

'He had certainly neither right nor reason to be.'

'Oh, come, Miss Pascoe. You may not have accorded
him the right. But if I were his age and—'

'If you were his age, so would I be,' Elspeth said.

Kenworthy came back to business.

'Obviously, various policemen will have turned your

flat upside down.'

'Not nearly as destructively as I feared that they might. After all—things must have looked fairly easy to them.'

'May I ask if your phone remained out of order?'

'No, it didn't. One of the policemen used it on arrival. It only struck me later that that was odd.'

'It's what I would have expected. Miss Pascoe, I would like to have a look at your flat. Elspeth and I would both like a look at your flat. Maybe we can help you to put things in order.'

That same evening a local league match was played between two club teams on the North Yorkshire coast. A pedestrianized shopping precinct in Great Driffield came off badly in the rampage that followed it. A copy of the somewhat helpless report was sent to Forrester's office.

It listed the shops that had been damaged and plundered.

Willy slipped out of the Buildings between eight and nine that evening. He loitered for some time outside the Navigation Inn, looking for some adult who would get him cigarettes for the Old Woman from the machine inside. His feet left the ground when his coat collar was lifted from behind. It was that big copper who had paid them a visit earlier that evening.

When Judith Pascoe returned to her office the next morning, her desk had a tidiness that could not have happened if somebody else had not been at it.

She knew she could hardly complain. The papers on which she had been working were Crown property, not hers. The top item on her morning's correspondence was a small, sealed envelope containing a one-line note. She was to present herself to the Deputy Secretary immediately on her arrival back. Killer Burton. She felt cruelly back in an old world.

Yesterday evening they had all three of them gone to Bishopswood Road. The Kenworthys did not need to be told her feelings about that flat. Nothing very clever about that — but she did know people who wouldn't have been so sensitive about it. Elspeth suggested a fundamental turn-round of furniture, and spotted in a jiffy how best it could be achieved. There was even hilarity about doing it, which did not seem contrived. There were enough pairs of hands to make easy work of dragging furniture about. But whenever anybody wanted to move anything, that always seemed to be the thing that Kenworthy wanted to be examining.

One thing to which he did give priority was the small junction-box where the telephone lead came in under a window. He called Judith over to look at it with him.

'Screw-driver scratch here. Ten seconds to disconnect. Equally easy to put you back in touch with the world. I'd say two men did what needed to be done in here. Twenty minutes gave them time enough — but I'm sure they did it in less. They wouldn't want to count their chances in minutes.'

'But how did they actually kill him? Can you *make* a man have a heart-attack that shows no other symptoms?'

'I know of no certain method — yet —'

'But there's some possibility — ?'

'Best not to worry your head about that. I promise you, some of the best authorities are going to be working on it. But I've met this syndrome before: something has happened that defies explanation. You're left with only one certainty: it has happened. So that's where we take it from.'

She had given Elspeth the go-ahead to stick her books back on the shelves as they fell to her hand. She would get them into some sort of order later. Aelfric's *Colloquy*; Cynewulfe's *Elene*; Hromond Grippson's *Saga*: the green boxfile containing her own work on Theo von Hvin. Was there now — had there ever been — any point in keeping all this? Kenworthy was emptying her wastepaper basket into the kitchen pedal-bin. She knew he was missing nothing. It was necessary, wasn't it? But he did not seem to be finding anything that impressed him. He was looking at nothing twice, setting nothing to one side. If he had brought out a lens to squint at something with, it would have looked like burlesque.

'The linen that was on the bed when you came back from the surgery — I suppose that was taken away?'

'The flat was swarming with CID. I didn't know who they all were. They stuck all sorts of things into plastic bags, gave me a receipt for it all. I can't say I checked it. And nothing's come back yet.'

'I'll look into that for you.'

'There's no hurry,' she said, with a hint of irony.

'If you feel like a few more questions?'

'Shall I get coffee going first?'

'Egham,' he said, when they were settled. There was a new order, a sense of fresh, possibly interesting angles about the flat, even if some familiar comfort had gone. She knew she'd be able to adjust to living here again. After they'd gone, she'd make a few minor adjustments.

'Egham: what did you really make of it?'

'Nothing firm. My job was just to convene it, manage it, see everything worked. The orders, the names of the delegates, the lecturers, the films to be borrowed — all came down from above.'

'Over those initials?'

'Mr Mather's. The files had been weeded of all previous minutes.'

'Is that usual?'

'If you're lucky. Percy had a name — quite unjustly, I now think — for phenomenal inefficiency. But he was always scrupulous about office formality.'

'Did you assume that he had initiated this conference?'

'No. To tell you the truth, I didn't think he had it in him.'

'And now you do think so?'

'I learned quite a lot about him at that dinner-table. I learned that he cared—cared very much—about what was going on behind the scenes. I felt that he was going to do something about it, cost what it may.'

'It appears that it may have cost him his life.'

'I've not really squared up to that till now.'

'Tell me, Miss Pascoe—'

'Judith. It's time we—'

'Tell me, Judith, do you *now* think that Percy Mather was at the bottom of Egham?'

'No.' She was firm on the point. 'He was too nice a man. There was a lot about Egham that was nasty.'

'You now think that he was not behind it because he was too nice. This time last week you did not think he was behind it because he was too inefficient. So you must have formed some notion, even without much evidence, as to whose baby it was.'

'I suppose so. I took it for granted it came out of the machine.'

'But it's a machine of which you know the shape and parts. And you have been working like a dynamo, trying to assimilate that machine.'

'All right, then, I'll plunge. Let's discount Sir Henry. I don't know whether he's as hopeless as he's made out to be. I'm not sure that any man could be. There are two Deputy Secretaries who keep the place functioning. Burton's a go-getter. He's said to live on a diet of Assistant Secretaries. When Burton starts chucking hammers about, people start looking to see where the lightning conductors are. Thompson is a very different genus. He smiles and always seems to be knee-deep in work. The division of labour is a bit vague. Burton is in charge of all matters concerning day-to-day running, establishment, personnel, commonplace aggro. Thompson does parliamentary reports, anything going out — or coming in. In point of fact there's an overlap. Burton makes anything his pigeon that drops into his line of vision. Thompson seems too good-natured to mind. Thompson—'

She hesitated. He urged her on.

'I've always thought of Thompson as a bottom-pincher: not that I've any cause for complaint. He looks the sort. If I were a young typist, I'd hug the wall if I had to pass him in a corridor.'

Elspeth had picked up a coffee-table folio of the *Book of Kells* and was turning its pages without ceasing to listen.

'So on balance, you're inclined to think that the conference was Burton's brain-child?'

'I assume that. I suppose I have always assumed that. I have no spectacular reason for doing so.'

'And you found the conference not to your taste?'

She had been categorical about it, but she gave it more thought now.

'Let me be careful. Don't let me create wrong impressions. The government has a right to be concerned with disorder. We are a department concerned with contingency planning — even if we are a bit of a laugh in Whitehall up to now. We'd be falling down idiotically if we didn't try to have something ready.'

'Even if it meant duplicating work done by other departments?'

'That happens. It ought to happen less than it does. I think we shall improve. I think Burton is determined we shall. And I believe Percy Mather, God bless him, had the same idea — in his way.'

'So where do you fall out with the conference?'

'Partly because I don't see on what criteria the

participants were selected. There was no one with power to speak for the General Staff. There was no one with any authority from the Home Office. We had one major-general, a divisional commander, two lieutenant-colonels of infantry, one Chief Constable, a man who has never brought himself to the public notice. And a bevy of retired policemen. I could do you a nominal roll from memory.'

'That would interest me.'

'What got me down was the relish they had for the nastier side of things. Water-cannon, plastic bullets, tear gas: there were men there who just don't see these things as expedients. They can't wait to be using them. Someone suggested using anaesthetic darts, as they do to catch wild animals. And when somebody said that anyone who fell asleep would be killed in the crush, they all laughed. There was a scene of nine men being hanged — super-imposed on settings of different English towns — Manchester, Malborough, Thame, Ripon, Leeds — places with a wide enough space. I don't really know why they showed that — except for the effect it had on some of the men. You could feel the surge. It was a sort of recurrent joke, running through the conference like a comedian's catch-phrase. There were men there who are dying for all that to happen.'

'They do exist,' Kenworthy said. 'When they were having the last Commons free vote on capital punishment, the Home Office was inundated with applications in advance for the job of hangman. You asked just now what the selection criteria were. I think you've said it all, haven't you?'

'In theory. I can't believe it's all true.'

'There are men who want it to come true. They were brought together in Egham. Elspeth — it's time we left this young lady to compose herself ready for tomorrow.'

★

Judith Pascoe did a short deep-breathing exercise at the window which gave her a less satisfying view of the Thames than Whippletree had. Then she picked up a clipboard and one ballpoint and made her way up to the Deputy Secretary's suite.

Killer Burton's ante-room was manned by one of those ageless PA's who fiercely protect their master — even when he is flailing destruction. As she flicked the switch on her panel to announce Judith, she knew what Judith was going in to get; and, unexpressively, she clearly asked no more of life than that Judith should get it.

Burton finished a minute with both archaic elegance and speed. Then his eyes looked out from under his brows and down his ploughshare of a nose. 'A falchion from its sheath' was the absurdity that crossed Judith's mind.

'Sit down, Miss Pascoe. You will understand that any attempt on my part to formulate a moral judgement would be quite *ultra vires*. It would be quite contrary to the spirit of personal licence of the age through which we are passing. If, therefore, you detect any distaste in my attitude, you will understand that that is purely personal. I cannot entirely rid myself of my faint lingering memories of those days when service of the Crown implied some sense of public decorum.'

She tried to make something of his room without appearing to allow her eyes to wander. Was there any sense of personality in it anywhere? There was plenty of work about: files stacked in every available space. But was there anything to suggest taste for anything but work? There were two pictures — a repro Canaletto and a derivative from Mondrian. These things circulated about government buildings; Burton had probably not noticed them. The only outside breath was a folded newspaper lying on a side-table with the crossword about a third done. It was one of Whippletree's. It was Whippletree's day. Did Burton even know whose brain was teasing him?

'You must clearly understand, Miss Pascoe, that no further research is to be undertaken by your section except by competent authority, and until such time as we have a new Under-Secretary, that means my authority. As it is, your section is obviously unemployed. Therefore all except your Senior Principal and two of your research assistants have been temporarily seconded to other sections. You and your remaining staff will work on one project, and one project only. The Tourist Board has asked us for a survey of changing demands for amenities at coastal resorts. You can get your section working on that straight away.'

Temptation: to fly off several handles, to challenge his dirty, needle-groove mind. She remained demure, not out of weakness, not because she was not heaving inside, but because every instinct was telling her to wait. And because anything she had to report would be grist to Kenworthy's mill.

'Yes, Mr Burton.'

'One other thing. Are there any other projects, so far undisclosed, on which this man Whippletree was working?'

'Not to my knowledge, Mr Burton.'

'Not to your knowledge? Well, now that your section is smaller, you will have less to get to know about, won't you? And at least you are free now of Whippletree.'

She wondered what section Peter Paul had been whipped away to.

'Free for all time,' Burton said. 'He has left without notice, having taken hysterical offence because a report on which he had no right to be working has been held up for interim evaluation. So you are permanently free of one problem.'

As she crossed the landing, she passed Thompson, the other Deputy Secretary, who was going somewhere with a file. He always seemed to be going somewhere with a file.

He gave her his wan smile. If she had been some temporary woman clerk, he would probably have sidled close past her. He did not look as if he had ever heard of the atrocities she was connected with: and yet he must have been in conference with Burton. She went back and sat at the alien tidiness of her desk. She stared at her phone. That instrument could be made to conjure up the human voice. But, she told herself firmly, not through the Duchy's switchboard. She slipped on her coat and took the lift down to the ground-floor, went round the corner to the call-box in Glansevern Street. There was no reply from Whippletree's home number. Why should there be?

CHAPTER 9

'So—you got neatly inside, and you helped with the furniture removing. Dust from the carpet showed traces of mud that could only have come from Epping Forest. All we need to find now is a Ford Cortina with a morsel of gravel in the tread that came from a garden drive opposite Highgate School.'

There was a touch of over-the-moon about Bransby-Lowndes, triggered by the self-satisfaction in Kenworthy's face. Kenworthy was in bouncing mood. He was not exactly keeping them waiting for the big news, but he was confident enough to be playing with them.

'Not quite,' he said, 'though I did find out quite a lot about Judith Pascoe. She's still not entirely convinced of her identity, you know. Well, that makes her sound a bit too much like a searching adolescent. I'm thinking about what she reads in bed—or tries to. Always two books at a time, reads alternate chapters, I think. She's still working her way through last year's Booker near-misses at the moment—but it looks as if the alternative is something that she feels she ought to be reading. At the moment it's by a woman called Garber on *Coming of Age in Shakespeare.*'

'Simon—we've all three of us passed through the stage of doubting Miss Pascoe's *bona fides.* Who followed her to her flat, taking Percy Mather with her, got in while she was fetching the doctor—having previously tampered with her junction-box—?'

'Someone who knew in advance she was going back to her flat, taking Percy Mather with her. Someone who knew that he was going to need a doctor—because he knew that Percy was going to feel ill. And it's no stride from there to say that he knew that because he had done something to make Percy feel ill.'

'Yes. I've not been able to think of a better theory than that myself. But get down to the dust from the carpet.'

'When Judith Pascoe moved into that flat, she was also moving from one government department to another; and nipping home for weekends with her parents to get her mother working on loose covers and curtains. She is a clean young woman, and she moved into a clean flat—but it was only surface cleanliness. She hoovered a fair amount of dust up—and shifted even more of it about. Now if you ask me about the diet of the previous inhabitants, or about the religious observances of those before them—'

'Simon!'

'No go. There were two men. I am convinced that there must have been two, who worked quickly, quietly, cautiously, undestructively—and in gloves, most probably surgical ones. They knew what they were doing, and had probably rehearsed it.'

'So we are no forrader?'

'Yes—we are. Percy and Judith dined Chez Festubert and left there by taxi. Now Chez Festubert isn't in the best of one-way systems if you're hanging about trying to wave down a cab. Therefore you'd ask the doorman to ring for one for you. And he'd have the number in his head, one of his wife's brothers, probably. Anyway, it would be likely to be a small firm from whom he got a regular cut. I proved to be right. Four-fifths of the cabs called to Chez Festubert are from Mainfleet, a medium garage in the Edgware Road. And I'm in luck, because some of the drivers have been suspected of working a racket—sheltering behind feigned radio breakdowns to do a spot of gentle moonlighting. So there's been rather a special effort lately, not to miss logging fares. Every evening last week, the boss's wife was sitting at the switchboard herself. And believe you me, when the drivers know she's on the net, they don't try anything.'

Kenworthy was still looking provocatively complacent.

'So I got the time, the place and the driver. One of the old school: woolly cardigan, hanging jowls and a no-lady-I'm-not-free-but-I'm-reasonable wit. He remembered Judith and Percy. Thought at first they were father and daughter, but went off that because he caught Percy giving her the old lovey-dovey look. Not a lot, though, because the old man was clearly feeling a bit rough. Kept closing his eyes, as if he had a nausea that wouldn't go away. He pretty well confirmed, in fact, Judith's own account—including helping Percy across the pavement, and the conversation about coming in for a drop of brandy. He didn't think there was any question of their making a dirty night of it, because the old man did look sadly past it.'

'But do we need all this confirmation, Simon?'

'More coming up. Our jowly friend did a U-turn outside Judith's place, because the boss's wife had despatched him on an immediate follow-up. And that's when he thought he saw a man hanging about, in the shadows of a garden hedge on the opposite side of the road. There's a wide curve, about twenty yards past Judith Pascoe's, and this character moved back towards a parked car round that bend. The cabby heard the engine start up as he straightened out and drove towards the main road.'

'Description?'

'Not helpful. Too shadowy and too standard. Not a young man, the cabby thought. Height about five ten. Active—not from the way he was slouching under the hedge, but from the way he moved towards the car. Jeans and a roll-necked sweater, the cabby thought. He didn't get a proper look at his face.'

'Doesn't quite narrow it down to one man, does it?'

'But—'

'Go on.'

' "Funny," the boss's wife said, "That was two fares from that French place to Highgate on the same evening." And she turned up another of her log-sheets. About a quarter to eight, a call from the doorman. That would be more or less when Judith and Percy were arriving for their meal, wouldn't it? Chap in early middle-age, still had an early Beatle-cut, and a moustache of that dejected Chinese style that makes so many men look alike these days. He wanted the Spaniards, on Hampstead Heath, only a few minutes' walk from Judith Pascoe's pad. But he didn't go straight in the pub. As the cabby—a different one—was turning in the forecourt, he saw him go to a parked car in which another man was sitting. Then they went into the pub together.'

'That all?'

'I admit that it doesn't get us *there*. But it gets us somewhere. We're panning in from Who? to Somebody. That's progress. I haven't seen Judith again yet. If she does happen to remember having seen somebody leave the restaurant—'

'*If*—'

Kenworthy looked at Bransby-Lowndes with a surge of impatience.

'You don't know what it's all about, do you — detection? There's an intolerable stage that we often have to go through — this breaking through from nobody to somebody. It may not look like progress — but it could be the biggest single step we have to take.'

'I don't think I could ever have stood your job,' Bransby-Lowndes said.

'Sometimes you don't even dare to hope. And when you do, you sometimes think you're still kidding yourself.'

'Forrester's pulled a line just about as far out of the water as you have,' Bransby-Lowndes said. 'Tell him, Forrester.'

Forrester had put his hand on Willy King's shoulder, scaring the life out of the kid. But that had not been enough to shake a useful story out of him. Willy was a sniveller, a physical weakling. He was destined to go slowly up the channels of do-goodery and correction until he ended up with manhood and his first prison sentence more or less in the same breath. Anyone could see that coming. But Willy was also essentially imitative. He knew how his father and brothers would have handled Forrester. They would have insulted him. Willy called Forrester a four-letter word that is a non-clinical term for the female pudendum. For a variety of reasons this riled Forrester beyond adult logic. He had been called the same thing before, by dangerous opponents, and had laughed at them when they said it. But coming from this little snot-gobbler, it opened a raw edge. Forrester's not inconsiderable hand was travelling through the air before he knew he was really going to hit the kid. He pulled back only just in the nick of time to save himself from doing lasting damage. As it was, his palm encompassed ear, cheekbone, left eye and nostril, rattling the lad's teeth in his jaw and sending the blood singing in his brain.

Somewhere behind him feet hurried past and away. Forrester brought the knuckles of his other hand into the flesh of Willy's arm, midway between shoulder and elbow, forcing him into the shadows of a railway arch that looked like a Doré illustration. *For God's sake watch it*, something was telling him: they had killed this little bastard's brother in Harwich.

But within the next minute or two, Willy was singing. Willy wanted no more of this. He could see this big sod serving him the way they had served Geoff.

Willy was not all that helpful. Through the blood and mucous that was running—not profusely—from his nose, he was ready to tell Forrester all he knew. But he did not know much. He would have told Forrester anything to please him—but he did not know what would please him. So he told what truth he knew, within the limits of his observation and memory. He told Forrester about getting parted from Geoff and Arfer at Gorleston, with an inflated description, as he had heard it, of Orangehead and Greenscalp. He told Forrester about the two blokes and about the lessons in kungfu and karate that they had promised Arfer. He told them about the meeting in Jimmy Maddock's gymnasium behind the Paki restaurant and, resentfully, how they had sent him home for the toilet-rolls, on purpose so he should miss the coach. Only he had got back in time; it was the bloke who had stopped him getting on. He gave a description of the bloke. It was rather less helpful than the cabby's description of the man on the forecourt of the Spaniards. Forrester was a highly experienced man at coaxing working descriptions out of inarticulate informers. But Willy was less than inarticulate. He had no yardsticks of age, class or complexion. He leaped hopefully to agree with every adjective that Forrester offered him, hoping each question would be the last. And Forrester was far from on form, still rattled with himself for losing his temper.

When he had finished with Willy, he had the conception of a man in his twenties, an inch or two under six feet, clean-shaven, longish but not overlong hair, chestnut duvet coat, cord trousers, blue and white canvas shoes. It did not exactly narrow it down to a few. It did no more than Kenworthy's drivers had done: it turned who? into somebody.

'You don't go back and tell your Old Man any of this. You do — and next time I see him, I'll tell him what you've told me. I'll tell him you grassed.'

Forrester went to see Jimmy Maddock in the gym behind the Pakis'. Jimmy was an ex-pug who ran a dying club for boys, in the hope of now and then pushing some promising kid lightweight into the promotions. Kids who had done a bit in the ring at school could come for 'training' — be taught how to make the most of the blind side of the ref. Jimmy lived in a daze of long-forgotten punches to his head, and had little more love for policemen than the Kings did. There had been a history of dubious relationships between him and a kid or two, and he had been harassed, but nothing had been proven.

Yeah, well, this was a new sort of supporters' club, Finsbury, wasn't it? These kids, they had to do something on their Sat'day arternoons. And the things that went on in the stands these days, they had to learn to use themselves, hadn't they? And this young fellow, he'd been round once or twice to fix up about hiring the place, but they hadn't got down to any proper training yet. Not a local, as far as Jimmy Maddock knew. Yes, of course he knew his name — Cartwright, Cartledge, something like that. Well spoken. Social worker of some sort, Jimmy wouldn't be surprised. Maddock gave a description which, on top of Willy's, reduced the man from one in five million to one in two million. How had Cartledge-Cartwright paid for the hire of the gym? By cheque? I should bleeding cocoa. Forrester had an idea that

Cartledge wouldn't be calling behind the Pakis' place again.

'Well, progress again,' Kenworthy said. 'When a man starts up a thing like this, he gets so far anonymously. He gets spotted, and he has to remember where not to show himself a second time. Sooner or later he has to stop showing himself altogether. I say again, we're thinking of *somebody* now.'

'We've got to move faster than this, Simon. We've got to assume that Mather was killed — if you can kill a man by inducing a heart-attack — because of something he knew. You'll be glad to know that the Yard are looking very unobtrusively at that angle now. Because one thing we haven't told you yet is that that stain on the bed-linen — Forrester's revolting map — isn't Mather's blood-group. You'll be even more pleased to know that the man doing the looking is your old friend Hewitson.'

'So what's the betting Whippletree will be next?' Kenworthy asked.

'Whippletree? Whippletree? Why Whippletree? All that's wrong with Whippletree is retarded adolescence. He's gone off now in a fit of sulks because a superior is quite properly sitting on one of his illicit reports.'

'Not so,' Kenworthy said. 'Do you think Whippletree cares two hoots about what goes on in Public Opinion polls?'

'He doesn't care about anything.'

'Maybe he does. He's turned in first-class reports in his time.'

'Have it your own way. Who's your informant? Judith Pascoe? She's only just met him.'

'Ask yourself,' Kenworthy said. 'If Percy Mather had information hot enough to get him craftily murdered, where did he get it from? Not from Judith: she's not been there long enough to know her way round. It must surely have been Whippletree. I'll grant you his cynicism. But hasn't the Duchy given him something to be cynical about? And Whippletree wouldn't be slow to realize, would he, that Mather had been got at. Even if he didn't know for certain, he'd wonder. So wouldn't he get himself out of harm's way — on a characteristic pretext — before the same thing happened to him? All right, don't believe me, if you don't want to, Bransby-Lowndes. But don't we at least stop and look at the likelihood? Or else stop talking about moving faster than this?'

'I'll settle for the possibility that Whippletree knows more about Mather's death than he ought to.'

'Then we must find him.'

'Why aren't you out looking?' Bransby-Lowndes asked.

CHAPTER 10

Judith Pascoe came to see the Kenworthys again; not to pose a single particular question, not to bring up a particular new problem. She needed someone to talk to. The treatment she had had from the Killer had upset her niche in the Duchy. She had called a meeting of the rump of III (Populace), had sown a few ideas for their new project. But none of them seemed to care much about the change of fashions at holiday resorts. Whippletree would have livened things up for them. She missed Whippletree. She had not come to the same conclusion about his disappearance as Kenworthy had, and Kenworthy had not set her thoughts in that direction. In a short time, she had got into the habit of using Whippletree as a baffleboard for her own thinking. Now she had no one to refer to. She was even worried about what he had done to jeopardize his career.

'It *is* possible to find missing people, isn't it?' she asked Kenworthy.

'It's frequently done. I'm not sure it's in the missing person's best interests, in every case. Your young friend is a free man, pursuing his own tastes. The Met wouldn't cancel any rest days to look for him. He hasn't committed any crime, has he?'

'There are some files missing.'

Kenworthy stopped chattering and asked a crisp question.

'What are they? Do you know?'

'My egregious Mr Burton is sitting very tightly on that information.'

'And you haven't been there long enough to have indiscreet contacts?'

She shook her head, Kenworthy yawned.

'I've always said—boasted, in fact—that I could find any man in London, if only I knew enough about him. Know the man, and you'll know where he'd go. But I've an idea that Whippletree might be a tall order. There'd be so much to know.'

'I wish you'd try.'

'Has he friends in the office?'

'He's civil with a great many. But they don't get beyond a certain point with him.'

'He must have worked closely with your research team. It's common ground that some of his reports have been extraordinarily good. You don't achieve that without excellent working relationships.'

'All that happened before my time in the building. Three-quarters of those people don't even work for me now.'

Kenworthy got up and went to his television set.

'Mind if we watch the News?'

Peaceful pickets, their slogans crude, but not really interfering with a royal walkabout; a shot-putter disqualified for suspected drug-taking; the escape of a snake from a private collector's suburban garden.

And then the violent spin-off of the evening's soccer. Harold Wood versus Dagenham at Dagenham. There were shots that were going to bleed the veins of some already pretty anæmic PR: constables looking like fascist para-military with face-shields and chin-guards, whaling into muscular tender spots with their riot sticks. There was no doubting that some of the rank and file were getting more pleasure out of it than they ought to be. But then, so were the cowboys. Beer-cans rolled emptily about tesselated shopping pavements, and these were being used to photogenic advantage. The window of a video-store had been stove in, apparatus lugged out and slammed against walls, cassettes splintered underfoot, yards of magnetic tape entangled about ankles.

One cameraman had had a keener eye for a shot than he had for the ethics of citizenship. He had tracked up on one of those who had got away, a lout classically poised to throw a half-brick through the window of an off-licence, just as a stray figure in uniform sprang at him from a doorway.

The vandal escaped. There was going to be a bitter claim in due course that a sound-engineer deliberately got in the way of the law—leaving it open to the camera to zoom in on the fugitive as he loped over the foundations and rubble-choked cellars of a clearance site.

It was not the morality of journalism that bothered Kenworthy: it was the fugitive himself. For there had been three seconds of well-defined profile—and there was no doubt about identifying Whippletree.

Judith Pascoe was pale.

'I'm sorry,' Kenworthy said, 'but we now have to re-examine some of our basic premises.'

'There was no mistaking him,' she said, without emotion.

CHAPTER 11

ILIFFE, Bernard Sykes, Ex Chief Inspector, Met. Uniformed branch in various divisions, interrupted by period as Inspector (Traffic) NSY. Voluntary early retirement before Yard purges. Reason given, domestic débâcle over unsocial hours, appears genuine. Uneventful career, undistinguished in any direction.

There was a new face at the front desk, unknown to Kenworthy, a man who did not know who Kenworthy was—which was insignificant. Why should anyone? This man had probably not even been a policeman.

Iliffe kept Kenworthy waiting. Higher Executive Officer—not a policy-maker of the Duchy. The lower they came in rank, the more self-importantly they insisted on their corridor-corner protocol. Come to that, the lower their rank, the more bloody work the poor sods had to do—and the less tolerable was it to have to give up half an hour to an unscheduled interview.

Up to the point of being shown into his room, Kenworthy had clung to a shred of hope that the sight of Iliffe might recall the man. The battle was half won if you had anecdotal common ground. But they were strangers, though Iliffe must have known Kenworthy by name.

When faced with Civil Servants, Kenworthy had often wondered, what the hell are they all worried about? In latter years he had known, though it had never been easy to put into words. It was just about the most difficult job in the world from which to get the sack. Before you got that far, there was always the Duchy of Axholme; yet they were all scared stiff of something. Maybe it was the fear of precipitating a change in the status quo, their own or somebody else's. He'd heard it said of one top-earner that he'd 'never put a foot wrong by dint of never putting a foot.'

One sight was enough for him to sum up Iliffe: the sobriety of a nearly new off-the-peg suit, his hair still cut to rookie shortness. No doubt he'd been an excellent man at spotting on the closed-circuit monitors where the next peak-hour snarl-up was going to be. Where it had been yesterday, for a certainty—but you waited for the build-up to be seen, before you wirelessed to the cars. As station inspector, night duty, he'd always have known when to refuse to accept a charge. And as chief security man at the Duchy, he'd maintain fair duty rosters (they were all round his walls), would know how to shuffle his jigsaw when a man was off sick; would be an admirable welfare officer to his men—as long as there was a precedent for any favour he was asked.

In the first twenty seconds, sitting in front of him at his desk, Kenworthy dismissed Iliffe as a force in anybody's land: from everybody's point of view a safe man, because he wore nowhere about him the menace of imagination.

Nevertheless, for a few minutes, Kenworthy went on trying.

'I don't think we ever did come across each other. I don't think I was ever pulled into one of your divisions.'

'I don't think so.'

'Weren't you at Sculthorpe Street when Sid Heather was DI?'

'We overlapped a month or two.'

'An old friend of mine was on your door duty the other day.'

'Oh?'

Iliffe was playing it so carefully that he even seemed to regard it as unsafe to admit the obvious.

'PC 496 Peters.'

'Ah yes.'

'Told me he was deserting the ship for Natsecure.'

Was it Kenworthy's suggestibility, or did the association touch a sensitive nerve in Iliffe? If so, he showed it not so much by a fidget as by a determined immobility, a rigid resolution not to be seen to react. Iliffe kept his eyes uninformatively fixed on Kenworthy's. Kenworthy charged on.

'What's the connection between this Duchy of yours and Natsecure?'

'I know of none. We've had one, two, three, four—' he counted them on his fingers—'four rank and file transfers out, of which Peters is the latest. Some of the conditions are made to seem marginally better.'

'Including pension?'

'Natsecure seems to have that covered.'

'Must cost them a pretty penny. You weren't at that conference at Egham where I talked?'

'I have nothing to do with that side of things. I'd looked the premises over, decided what strength of guard to send. May I ask, what's your—?'

'A watching brief, for Forrester.'

Iliffe had ample ways of knowing that, so why prevaricate? Iliffe did not reveal whether he already knew or not.

'Tell me more about Natsecure.'

'I don't know what there is to tell. These private agencies are mushrooming, as you well know. I can't think it's a good thing—though Natsecure has Commander Cawthorne behind it. You couldn't ask for a better guarantee than that, could you?'

'Couldn't you? And it's ex-Commander—'

Kenworthy meant it to sound iconoclastic. If Cawthorne was one of Iliffe's idols, then one had to start tearing into him at some point or other to see what would happen. Iliffe's back went up—not because he was playing a role, but because he wasn't in the habit of being contradicted.

'I suppose you were nearer to him at the Yard than I ever was,' he said at last.

'There are one or two others, aren't there—Walter Kershaw, D.D. Bragg, Sam Tyrrell?'

At one time, those names had been the subject of a new latrine-rumour every day.

'I never knew much about that side of things,' Iliffe said. 'I know there were smears. Careers were ruined without charges being brought.'

'Mark got rid of nearly three hundred officers in the mid-'seventies,' Kenworthy said.

'I got on with my own job and didn't worry myself over other men's troubles.'

Iliffe had become very uneasy indeed. Then suddenly Kenworthy wanted to laugh. There were some, very close to the heart of things—Forrester for one, Bill Clingo, Shiner Wright—who had known that Kenworthy had resigned in disgust. There were others who had got hold of the wrong end of the stick. And Iliffe had to be one of that bunch, hadn't he—the crowd that believed that Kenworthy too had been given the option to get out or else? Kenworthy's pride being what it was, that had always riled him—riled him even more than the heights that Cawthorne had scaled. Cawthorne and company.

'So look, Kenworthy, I'm a busy man. If you tell me where your interest lies, what your precise authority is, and ·what it is you want to know—if it lies within my province and my terms of service—'

It was at that moment that Kenworthy decided that Iliffe was feeble and genuine. There had to be a security man at Millbank, and his duties were straightforward. He was chief watchman, that was all. He wasn't here as a tool for Cawthorne, Kershaw, Bragg and friends. He wasn't sharp enough by half to be of any use to that lot. Iliffe was here as a straight man. It was good for any crooked unit to have a few straight men about.

So Kenworthy decided to round this meeting off and let his feet find their way to a few more offices in this building, Judith Pascoe's, for example. Iliffe's telephone put an end to talking, anyway. Its sudden ring startled Iliffe: the underlying tension really was pathetic.

He lifted the receiver and listened to a spate of words in increasing unease that he could not hide. He was getting what the army used to call a rocket, seemed to have no armament against the barrage that was smiting his eardrums. About his normal work, at least half his mental capacity must be absorbed in having excuses ready in advance: but this salvo seemed to have him off his guard. He drew a jotter towards himself and seemed to draw comfort from noting down detail.

'Yes, Mr Burton—but you can't expect me to know till I've gone into it. We do carry out regular snap-checks, but I can't have a man on hand every time a file is booked out to a branch.'

Security of access to classified records would be part of his responsibility. There'd be an official drill, and he'd have to see they stuck to it. But it was not uncommon for a department to get laxer and laxer, as men cut corners—until the next periodic earthquake. Now, of course, files had disappeared: Whippletree was said to have taken some with him. Iliffe was paid to bear the brunt when Burton was on this warpath. And Burton was living up to his reputation, for no doubt the official channel, if Burton wanted Iliffe ticked off, was for him to go down through Iliffe's own PUSS. But where Burton wanted to go, he went direct. The whole Duchy was the Killer's pigeon.

'Yes, Mr Burton, I'll report back to you as soon as I know.'

And then Iliffe did more listening, in which he was obviously being asked more questions—to which he did not seem to care to give direct answers.

'A man called Kenworthy,' he said at last. 'Yes, sir—I'll bring him up to you myself—straight away. One of our Deputy Secretaries would like to speak to you,' he told Kenworthy.

There were some files at any rate that were not missing. They were in Killer Burton's room in stacks—stacks on his side-tables, stacks in the corners, stacks by the skirting-boards, stacks on trolleys, stacks on his desk. And Burton's hurricane activity, the unsheathed falchion of his eye, his bulldozer of a nose, presided over this fecundity of documents, obviously knowing where every scrap of paper in this chaos was.

'All right, Iliffe, you can leave us to it.'

Burton was like the mate of a Horn-thrusting windjammer. He knew the state of every knot on shipboard. But behind the bolts of their cabin-doors, even hard-case mates had been known to read books, to write letters, to play hymn tunes on mouth-organs. And there was another side to Burton's character, that no one had told Kenworthy about—perhaps because no one knew. Burton came round his desk, shook hands with Kenworthy, took Kenworthy to sit in a leather armchair in a window alcove with a view of the river broader even than Whippletree's. And Burton opened his window a fraction and cast out to the pigeons a few crumbs of crust from his breakfast toast. His voice as he spoke to Kenworthy was not hearty—not quite as contrary to popular report as that—but it was *legato*, a cultured voice, the voice of an unflappable commander. Kenworthy wondered whether this was perhaps the Killer at his most lethal, the assassin about to strike. He had had a commanding officer like that during the war. When he smiled at you, you started getting worried. If he called you by your Christian name, you started thinking who could be the prisoner's friend at your court-martial.

'You don't remember me? I didn't think you would. I don't think we spoke—'

'You mean at Egham? I don't think I saw you there.'

'No. I wasn't. For a variety of reasons, all carefully calculated—and some of them no doubt totally misguided.'

Blunt-instrument sarcasm? It seemed not. The Killer seemed quite happy to admit his fallibility.

'No. I was at Sydenham Rotary when you first gave your talk. Do you realize that that was upwards of thirty-five years ago? I was very much out in the field in those days, stuck in an office in Croydon. Rotary seemed an oasis of sanity—that's some measure of the sort of life I was leading. Yes: I heard your talk. That's why you were invited to address our little circus overlooking the Thames Valley. I thought you'd come in with the right brand of innocence. So now you're with Bransby-Lowndes? You're wasting your time, you know, trying to get anything out of Iliffe. The man would be more at home minding a brazier by a hole in the road. Early days yet, I suppose, for you to update me as to what you've found out?'

'I seem to be finding something contradictory every few minutes.'

Burton grinned, and it was not even a sinister grin—not the baring of teeth about to gnash a man to ribbons.

'Contradictory about me, do you mean?'

'Opinions do seem to differ.'

'They are meant to. Keep 'em guessing. Perhaps I had better make one thing clear before we go on. I have one aim in this life. That is to pull this department out of the music-hall custard-pie throwing act that it was when I came here, and turn it into something worth having on a government's payroll. Axholme, of course, was all codswallop. We only made one decision in the whole of that phase of our existence—and the courts overturned it.

I'm sorry to say that when we started the contingency planning concept, the element of farce still persisted in many quarters. But the dross keep departing. We are getting fresh blood. Your friend Miss Pascoe, for instance. I take it she's wept it all out of herself on to your shoulder? The tale of my latest atrocities? I just had to rid that section of hers of anything with its roots in the old days. She'll be able to build up from there.'

'And what about Whippletree?'

Burton took a deep breath — and concentrated for a moment on an orange-eyed pigeon.

'The biggest fool that even the Duchy has ever had — and I'm ˈeven counting Bessemer. Because Bessemer never did have anything in him. But I'm not saying that that makes Whippletree our inside villain. He could be. I could just as emphatically say that he couldn't be. Whippletree is a man of immature principle: that's why I don't think he'd play along with Natsecure. But immature! So capable — and yet so incapable of putting himself consistently to any useful purpose. That thing he did about Opinion Polls was superb, quite superb. But it was beyond him to know that the time for it is not now: that with the constituencies talking in terms of snap-election, any government, of any party, would simply slip the skids from under us. They'd wind up the Duchy if they knew at this stage that this report even exists. But the Whippletrees of this world never see the benefit of waiting for anything. But needless to say, it's only a cadet branch of even the Whippletrees, a sub-genus, that goes off in a huff and throws up an established job for the sake of a principle. Well, he'll have done for himself as far as the Civil Service Commissioners are concerned. And I shan't fight his cause for him. If my life has taught me anything, it's that the most useful people you have around you are those who'll make a bloody nuisance of themselves from time to time. But Whippletree has run amok just once too often for this child.'

He did not seem to know anything about the brick-throwing incident. Could there be other things about Whippletree that Kenworthy knew and Burton didn't? Whatever one made of the paradoxes of Killer Burton, there was no way of knowing what he would tell the truth about. Kenworthy had an idea that *truth*, for Killer Burton, was just another device that might occasionally have its tactical uses. So he saw no point at this moment in revealing something that Burton might not know. It seemed vital to steer the talk away from Peter Paul Whippletree.

'And what about Percy Mather?' he asked.

'Oh, they killed him,' Burton said, as casually as if he were pronouncing the demise of a file. 'Very cleverly, I think. At least, he seems to have obliged them by dying of natural causes: as he was likely to do, it seems, from minute to minute of the last twenty years. One can only assume that if his timing had not been so convenient, they would have to fall back on ingenuity. One assumes that they went to Miss Pascoe's flat equipped for more than one type of emergency. After all, they must have taken pyjamas to dress the corpse in and some revolting sort of phial with which to stain the bedclothes. I take it that there must be something that can be applied with a hypodermic needle that produces the illusion of a heart-attack. And either the pathologist was too damned idle to find evidence of it—or they didn't need to use it.'

Burton seemed to take this for granted. He might have been talking of a monthly requisition for office stationery.

'Of course, the *modus operandi* is more in your line than mine. I don't even need to know about it.'

'Who?' Kenworthy asked, as soon as he could get the word in.

'Natsecure, obviously. I wouldn't have thought you'd have needed me to tell you that.'

Burton's eyes narrowed. The warhead of his nose took tentative aim. It was a momentary flashback to the Killer of repute, suddenly suspecting inefficiency in a quarter in which he had been reposing unreasonable hopes.

'I just wanted to hear you say it,' Kenworthy said, inspired.

'It hardly needs saying, does it? Natsecure—staffed and *owned* by senior retired policemen with records that one might charitably call dubious—has been using the Duchy—'

The murder of PUSS, Investigation Branch, was something, it seemed, to be taken with aplomb. But the effrontery of using the Chancelry—!

'They have used the Duchy as an intelligence agency for getting at facts, figures and trends in government thinking. They have used us to gain introduction to key personalities. Like a certain major-general who prays on his knees every night that next time it will be his division that is called in to reinforce the civil authority. Like getting on drinking terms with two Chief Constables who are hoping against hope that the next outbreak will be on their territory.'

'In other words, they have had active connivance within your own walls. Very active connivance indeed.'

Burton returned uncompromisingly to his Killer image.

'I'm glad that your reason for being here is beginning to dawn on you.'

'You've been here throughout. Ought you not to be a stage ahead of me?'

Burton subsided.

'I ought. I ought. I grant you I ought. All I can say with any certainty is that Mather came to me with documents that had come carelessly into his hands. Every organization is at the mercy of its clerks. Someone had made a bad job of cleaning up a file. We defused the Egham conference in the light of what that file told us. It was to have been no less than an operational planning session—to prepare, to provoke, to mount and then to quell a civil commotion. They would have made Brixton look like playground football.'

'And they really believed that if they could restore order, they could remain in semi-permanent command?'

'Not on your life! Wherever did you pick up that fantastic notion?'

Burton looked at Kenworthy as if he doubted his basic intelligence.

'That's not it at all. It isn't government they want. They're not as mad as that. It's Natsecure they want to put on the map. Let there be an urban battle. Let it be fought by vandals, racists, anarchists, trots, strikers, unemployed, anyone who's handy. Let it rage as long as a week. Let the army be called in and overdo it. Let a trigger-happy police force alienate every parlour-liberal in the country. Let property-owners start shitting themselves. Then let Natsecure pull something out of the bag—perhaps even negotiate a truce. Frightening—and not all that fantastic.'

'Maybe now that so much has been rumbled, Natsecure will have second thoughts.'

'They can't afford to. They're too much in debt. They had to go to merchant bankers to get themselves going. They had to renew their loan, because they didn't get going. The bank thought it better to double their stakes than lose what they'd already put in. But there's no more where that came from. They've bought in a few hundred former policemen. The terms had to be attractive, even extravagant. Natsecure needs contracts—and there's a lot of competition in the field. They need protection contracts—and not just from small traders. From leading insurers. That's where the big returns lie. Kenworthy, it's common knowledge that you worked alongside the men who are now on the Natsecure board: Cawthorne,

Kershaw, Bragg, Tyrrell—'

Kenworthy chose not to be tempted. On that subject he had chosen not to be tempted by less dangerous men than Burton. He had even spared Elspeth the hard core of it.

'What about this man you replaced by Miss Pascoe?' he asked. 'Former head of Section III (Populace)?'

'Bessemer? Round the twist. Had been ever since we won him from Social Security. That's why we won him from Social Security. Thinks he's a teapot.'

'Useful for a certain genre of Civil Service joke, anyway.'

But there were times when one doubted whether Burton had a sense of humour.

'I was speaking figuratively, of course,' he said. 'Count Bessemer out of your calculations. Bessemer was pure Duchy—original Duchy. Look: I'd like you to meet one or two other people while you're here. We might even catch Sir Henry—although I do know he's off to a viewing at Sotheby's sometime this morning.'

CHAPTER 12

Was it odd that Kenworthy's first glimpse of Ted Thompson should be a mirror-image of how everyone described him? Young middle-aged, contriving by some combination of boyish feature and trendiness to look even younger than that. He was not trendy in any outlandish sense: trend-conscious rather than trend-obsessed. But he clearly spent a lot on his clothes. Today he was wearing a velvet jacket, mushroom toned, with widely flared trousers. He had a lot of hair, that threatened to get out of hand every minute and never did. He was going somewhere when Kenworthy saw him—coming out of a door, going towards a door. With a file and a smile. A smile and a file, that was Ted Thompson, and you did not have to look at him twice to believe the tales about his being a slap-and-tickle merchant: a harmless slap-and-tickle merchant. God knows that he thought his purpose in life was: to bring pleasure to the lives of those he slapped and tickled, most probably. He smiled, Gioconda-wise, at Kenworthy, as he might have smiled at a passing typist — or Judith Pascoe. He even had a smile for Killer Burton.

The door for which he was heading was Sir Henry's. Piloted by the Killer, they all went through it together. Sir Henry, abundant white hair, sixtyish, retired military appearance — cultivated (he was not retired military) — was looking at a Catalogue of Sale, but not with concentration. One felt that he had just picked it up, the moment before his door opened. The moment before that, he had been doing nothing at all.

Yet he seemed to know all about Kenworthy. There was none of the uphill slog that one had been led to expect, trying to get through to him, staying through to him, getting him to understand what it was all about.

'Ah yes — you're with Bransby-Lowndes, eh? Come to sort us out, have you? Shouldn't think it will take you long. Find that blessed young Whippletree for us. Thursday's his day. Always know his style, you know. Not so many blessed anagrams as they give us some days. Can't stand too many anagrams. Get on my nerves. Do you think he'll be able to keep it up from wherever he's swanned off to? I dare say we'll be all right for a bit. His editor probably keeps a few weeks in hand.'

Then he turned to Burton.

'Glad you brought Kenworthy up. He can stay and listen to what Ted's got to tell us. Lord Downes is coming in at ten-thirty. The Vice-Chancellor too. In case there's a whisper. Thank God there's been no leak so far. No questions down yet, but there will be. And people come sidling up to them in the library, the members' tea-room, wanting to know. Believe you had them hanging on your lips at Egham, Kenworthy.'

Kenworthy saw a new version of this picture. Sir Henry Woodcroft's besetting sin in Forrester's notes had been laziness — not just procrastination, not just a shuffling of uninviting papers to the bottom of his box, but a consummate laziness, an accomplishment of laziness, backed up by the conviction that if his staff pushed a case for decision in front of his eyes often enough, over a long enough period — if, in fact, it would not go away — then it might, in the long run, be worth applying himself to.

But this did not mean, ultimately, incompetence. Far from it. 'Fearing and resenting any show of energy, enthusiasm, conscience or ambition in others.' That, after all, had been the report of the department anxious to be rid of him. When Sir Henry did move himself, he had a quick grasp, a vivid recall and undeviating intent.

'Hope these beggars aren't going to stay till lunch-time.'

'No, sir,' Thompson said. 'Lord Downes is meeting American friends of his wife at the Dorchester and Hersholt has an appointment with constituents.'

'So let's hear what we are going to tell them, Ted.'

Thompson's smiling, filing role in the Duchy was now clear. He collated what was worth collating from the eighty-five per cent rubbish that was turned out in this building and made it presentable for those who were entitled to have it presented to them. Ted Thompson looked after the outgoings. An effective team, in fact: Burton to see that the cogs turned, Thompson to select and collect the produce, Sir Henry to hand it over with due cere-mony, Lord Downes and Hersholt to answer to the public when all means of avoiding that had failed. (And somewhere in the background, the likes of Percy Mather, Judith Pascoe and Whippletree, trying to anticipate.)

They were still chatting amiably when the figureheads of the legislature arrived. Lord Downes was a surprisingly young man, who had succeeded to the third barony within the last five years, his grandfather having subscribed generously to party funds from the proceeds of definitive pioneering in the early aircraft industry; never mind which party. Hersholt was a trim, silent man in a dove-grey waistcoat and silver-sheened tie.

They talked for five minutes about Montpellier faïence, Downes having bought two Estevé drug-jars the previous week. Then it was his lordship who brought them down to business. Kenworthy, it having been strongly stressed that he was one of the inner circle, was empthatically pressed to stay.

'Now, Henry, what's this damned cabal you're fostering?'

Sir Henry did the answering. Thompson stood smiling by, ready to prompt. Burton had hardly spoken since they came into the room.

'Perfectly simple. We always keep a weather-eye on possible unrest.'

'Quite proper. One of the things we are here for.'

'We held a working conference. Thompson will give you a memo of dates and personalities. Police, army, retired police with inside experience. We updated ourselves, got a few new angles, compared systems.'

'Are they likely to say it's the nucleus of a para-military?'

'Tell them that's balderdash.'

'Theoretical readiness for an emergency, then.'

'There are bound to be some, of course, who don't even want us to be ready.'

'And did I hear a buzz that a young man's disappeared taking files with him? If the press get hold of that . . .'

'He's on sick leave. Overwork.'

'Is there or is there not any connection between all this

and the character who died up in Highgate?'

Lord Downes's insistence was acute. Any real clash of interests between him and Sir Henry could lead to radical changes. But it would never come to that. On the long horizon there was no clash of interests.

'No connection,' Sir Henry said. 'If we have to get uptight about it, private lives are of no public concern. After all, no one was involved who matters. The old chap seems to have overdone it in the love-nest.'

'How about the woman in the case?'

'Discretion in person. She daren't not be.'

'And what really happened?'

'We don't know yet.'

'It would surely be better not to.'

'For as long as we can.'

There was nothing in the style of it that was new to Kenworthy—but it was an impressive confirmation of something that he had always believed. Titles; an elite; a kid-gloved façade; wealth. But you were fooling yourself if you thought that these people were idle, or slow-witted, or incompetent. It didn't follow because a man had had it made for him that he wasn't up to it. They might have cohorts to do their work for them. But if it came to the crunch, if they felt like exerting themselves, you couldn't guarantee that they wouldn't still be leading the field.

It was pleasant, ten minutes later, to be at river level, a gull resting for seconds in a choppy trough, the defective public address system on a water-bus naming buildings that tourists would have forgotten in a minute and a half.

Kenworthy walked across Parliament Square towards Forrester's office. He always got a weird sort of kick out of having the seat of government casually around him. He had been aware of it in wartime, on leave. Sandbags in Whitehall had been where it all started and stopped: brewed-up tanks in North Africa, SOE, convoys assembling offshore off estuaries—Alamein, Lofoten, Chindits—

This morning a busload of Germans were craning their necks at the statue of Charles I. A provincial bevy was clustering outside St Stephen's: Hersholt's constituents? An LTE bus was heading for Old Ford. A uniformed messenger was coming out of a side-door of the Home Office carrying an historic old red despatch-box. His lunch, probably. A black security van was driving up to the limit past the Cenotaph. Not Natsecure.

Somewhere in the provinces—something vital was prompting Kenworthy that it would happen within the next fortnight—somewhere in a high-rise wilderness, or on a grid of squatters' terraces—something was going to snap. It was going to snap because someone was going to snap it. A few dozen people's homes were going to be gutted. There were going to be deaths that nobody intended. Weeping women would be observing disorientated ethnic rites. Rabble-rousers would be whipping up hatred of a coroner who was doing his best. Kids were going to be hurt, the wrong man's head stove in. Small businesses were going to be wrecked. Shop windows were going to be looted. It would be blamed on successive governments, Enoch Powell, Idi Amin, the Unions, investment in Korea, the EEC, West Indian carnivals, Japanese imports . . .

It would settle down eventually—until next time. Everyone would be just that little worse off than they were before it started.

Except—if things went their way—for Cawthorne, Walter Kershaw, D.D. Bragg, Sam Tyrell . . .

CHAPTER 13

'They love working to formulae, you know, these people. Proven notions — a sudden familiar juxtaposition of words or ideas — '

'These people' meant government. Bransby-Lowndes was pontificating, in the quiet drawl that went for pontificating with Bransby-Lowndes. 'What they are looking for — what will scare them stiff — what they ask me about every morning — is an unlikely combination. Ever since Paris, 1968 — *because* of Paris, 1968. Did you ever notice how coy the French middle class used to be when they talked about the Events of 1968? *Les événements* — there's something coy about the word itself; just as in the Middle Ages the word *peste* was an obscenity. Because in 1968, it was *Aux Barricades!* — a phrase they've heard in Paris just once too often. And what had gone wrong in Paris this time, what no one had predicted, was a bizarre combination. The students had suddenly thrown their hands in with the trade unionists. That's why there were barricades again, down by the Ecole des Mines. And at the first suspicion here that two militant factions that don't usually know one another — '

Forrester moved his coffee cup away from a tottering tower of paper.

'We've had nothing suggestive of that in yet — except for a minor scrap on Tees-side. And we've eyes and ears everywhere.'

'It's the adjourned Parkeston inquest today. Anything moving that way?'

'We know that the Kings are going to be there — with a neighbourly support-group, and the local Civil Rights lobby. There may be a bit of untidiness. The local police

are hoping to be diplomatic. They don't really expect
trouble. They're saying that Harwich is a long way for
people to go. It isn't near any disaffected conurbation.
Colchester doesn't worry them, and there's not been
much noise from Ipswich. And what have you to report,
Kenworthy? How are the blossoms of the Duchy blowing?'

'They've ruffled up their feathers and tucked their eggs
snugly up under themselves.'

'Funny way for blossoms to behave.'

'I mean, they go on hoping they'll have nothing to
answer for. When they do, they'll pay out their answers
slowly, very slowly—days after the questions. Something
may collapse. They'll live in last-minute hope that it
won't.'

'And what's your next move?'

'Find Whippletree.'

'That idiot. You know what I think? I think he tried to
get himself arrested to see if they'd treat him the way they
treated the King boy.'

'For a man who wanted to get himself arrested, he ran
fast enough not to be.'

Forrester broke in. 'We've been watching his Chelsea
flat. He hasn't been home.'

'He won't have been.'

'So where do you even start?' Bransby-Lowndes asked.

'Favourite pubs. Casual pals.'

'Get you nowhere. Whippletree can live without places
and people.'

'It would be criminal neglect on our part to assume
that.'

'All right. If you think you have the time.'

'Then there's the girl. I don't know how he feels about
her. I think he's at least interested. She might be good
bait.'

'But how are you going to get anything to him? I must
tell you here and now that any message on the box,

anything in the papers — even the most cryptic of hints — is absolutely ruled out. We want no press guns firing.'

Kenworthy paused to look at him bitterly. The Faculty was perhaps the most elite, potentially one of the highest-powered inquiry agencies in the world. But in his relatively short association with it, Kenworthy had met more frustration, more outright prohibition, than in most of the other set-ups in which he had worked. In this instance, Bransby-Lowndes was right. Let the press get in on this, let them start anticipating barricades, let them scent Natsecure, and fatal frontier incidents would not be long delayed.

In any case, why not enjoy a moment's sentimentality? There was an English way of doing things that had been winning last battles for centuries.

The English way of doing things? Did that mean Lord Downes, Ted Thompson, Sir Henry Woodcroft?

'So?' Bransby-Lowndes was asking him.

'There's another bait. I'm going to ask you to play it for me — it's more in your line than mine. Whippletree's crosswords: if I know the man, it's the one thing in his life that he wouldn't like to fall down on — other things being equal. He had his first in print when he was sixteen — was on the regular setters' panel within eighteen months. I doubt if he's ever missed a deadline. There must be some sporadic contact for his competition editor's queries and suggestions.'

'That's a long way from finding him.'

'It's a possibility. I know of no other.'

'He can post his copy in without giving an address.'

'Don't let us turn back before we've started. Let's try.'

How the hell did these prudent buggers ever get anything done?

'It seems to me the old objection applies. It's an approach through the press.'

Kenworthy laughed. 'That's why I'd rather you did it

than me. You'll go in at the top, muttering "Cabinet." '

'What exactly do you want me to ask for?'

'Not Whippletree's whereabouts. They'd be bound to jib at that. There's something sacrosanct about a man's address. They're always afraid that they'll get somebody on to a junk-mail circulation list. But try to get something up. Even a meeting with his crossword editor in a pub might give us a few clues. Ha-ha.'

'The crossword editor is probably a part-time amateur like himself. Maybe some vicar in the wilds of Cumbria. I don't see why he should know where we can find Whippletree.'

Bransby-Lowndes looked uncertain, ruminated, then became unexpectedly cheerful.

'I'll try. And what follows Whippletree?'

'Cawthorne,' Kenworthy said. 'Sometime Commander. Watler Kershaw, D.D. Bragg, Sam Tyrrell — and one or two lesser lights from the same spawning-ground.'

There was a short and telling silence.

'This is the moment you've been waiting for for years, isn't it, Simon?'

'On the contrary. Everything in me seems to want to put it off. I *am* putting it off — from day to day.'

'Isn't it about time you unbuttoned a lot of history for us?'

But Bransby-Lowndes was not being very pressing. Forrester knew better than to say anything at all.

'Shift-oh,' Bransby-Lowndes said, his slang as remote from the present world as ever.

'I'll leave a message for you downstairs after lunch, if I've any news on the crossword front.'

CHAPTER 14

The Old Woman seemed to have developed an Old Woman's thing about football. The Kings were unprepared for the storm that greeted Willy's appearance in a Finsbury supporter's scarf just as they were belatedly ready to move off to the inquest at Parkeston. They were to travel, with a miscellany of others, in a clapped-out minibus that belonged cooperatively to the squatters in Ushant Terrace. Already the driver was hooting Woody Woodpecker rhythms on the forecourt of the Buildings. And there was Willy, with the orange and green stripes of a Finsbury scarf wound round his neck, its tassels reaching down below his knees. The Old Woman did her nut.

She had done a lot of thinking about the respect due to a coroner's court. She ran to unwind the scarf from Willy as he was unwinding it from himself, thereby nearly losing a second son by strangulation. It was only when the Kings reached ground level that she saw that everyone in the minibus was wearing Finsbury colours. She charged back up four flights of stairs to bring her brood in line with the rig of the day. Willy was the only one left without. He had to make do with a measly rosette, and snivelled about it all the way through Stratford, Ilford, Romford and beyond.

The opening of the inquest earned no more than a few seconds' reference on *The World at One*. There had been a small pavement demonstration as the coroner mounted the steps of the building, some singing and chanting in the street during the first hour of whatever was going on inside. The local police were keeping a low profile — and a high state of reserve.

*

Kenworthy studied a run-down of the Board of Natsecure.

Chairman: Francis Windop Cawthorne.
Directors: Walter William Kershaw (Managing) Donald Davies Bragg (Operations) John Brimicombe Tyrrell (Personnel) David John Bellamy (Publicity)
Secretary: Allen Weston Dykes
Treasurer: Simeon Richardson.

Plus a statutory list of bankers, solicitors and accountants.

By company law, all this information had to be publicly available. And Kenworthy had no difficulty in reconstructing from memory the state of the hierarchy as it had been when he had been closer to it.

METROPOLITAN POLICE FORCE
L(Y) (Special Reference) Department
Deputy Assistant Commissioner: J.B. Tyrrell
Deputy Director: W.W. Kershaw
Principal: A.W. Dykes
Commander: F.W. Cawthorne
Chief Superintendent: D.D. Bragg
Superintendents: D.J. Bellamy, S. Richardson

There had been other names, of course, a few more Principals, some lesser lights, a pair of hard-pressed Inspectors. But they did not count. They had been there at the front, to help to keep the thing respectable — and to get on with the humdrum work. There had always been an air of portentous mystery about L(Y) Department — but that was not in itself sinister. In an organization as complex as the Met, and faced with the inside problems that the Met couldn't help having, there had to be a section to find answers to tricky questions: the sort of tricky answers that came easily to men like

Kershaw and company. In the early days one hundred per cent of their official work—and ninety per cent of all they did—was legitimate. It was L(Y)'s job, for example, to know when the Force was being hamstrung by its own regulations—and what needed to be unblocked. It was only when outsiders were called in to investigate the Yard that L(Y) found fresh fields. They became a sort of phantom, going over independently—and in consummate secrecy—the cases that the strangers were looking at. It was suspected by some that they were even going over the strangers—with equal secrecy. They kept ahead of outside investigators. It was rumoured that they sometimes sequestrated evidence, grew hedges round witnesses. All in the good name of the Yard—some said. The Yard was quite capable of putting its own house in order. They did not need outsiders. There was nothing wrong at Scotland Yard that L(Y) could not ferret out—and do something about.

And that was not all they did.

It was ironical that at the time of vintage L(Y), Commander Cawthorne had been answerable to Walter Kershaw and Sam Tyrrell. Even Dykes had not been far below him, salary-wise. But Cawthorne had always known how to exercise command upwards as well as downwards. It depended on what you could find out about people. As a detective-sergeant, way back in the 1940's, it had been rumoured that he was blackmailing his own DI.

It would be the easiest thing, this very afternoon, to go and chat them up at Natsecure: to drop in on Allen Dykes, to be taken across the corridor for a hearty, hyopcritical handshake with Donald Bragg and Sam Tyrrell. If he didn't go soon, Bransby-Lowndes would start pushing him. But every instinct in Kenworthy was still for putting it off.

He did put it off.

*

The inquest on Geoffrey King made the early evening
news bulletins, but not with much wealth of information.
There had been some disturbances within the court-
room. The coroner had clearly exercised — had been told
that he must exercise? — patience out of the ordinary. But
he had at one point had to threaten to clear his court. In
the end he had adjourned the proceedings to enable other
witnesses to be located. That was after the greenly
inexperienced solicitor representing an amateurish
community association had tried to sub-poena the
production of documents from the internal police
inquiry.

In effect the coroner was a pensive, kindly and
supremely dutiful man, with no more pomp that was
appropriate to his respect for any class of dead. Even in
cases where he knew the bereaved had bad consciences,
they were susceptible to grief and shock. He was always
thoughtful on behalf of the bereaved. But it was hard to
comfort the grief of Albert King, who wanted to make
statements and ask not-so-clever questions the moment
they came into his head: a man who would not listen to
the solicitor who was trying to help for nothing. Albert
King had a slanging match with the solicitor while a main
police witness was in mid-answer.

The evidence was tangled. There had been a mêlée in
the railway waiting-room that had been used as a
clearing-house. The memories of policemen, of Finsbury
fans, of skirmishing pacifists were chaotic, charged not
only with what they had seen, but with what, ever since,
they had talked about having seen. The police, at least,
had undergone the discipline of a formal statement of
evidence not long after the affray. The other witnesses
had worked unwittingly on each other. Two people *knew*
that Geoff King had been hit at the back of the skull
with what looked like a pick-axe handle. But it was

persuasively demonstrated by others that they could not possibly have been standing anywhere near where they could have seen such a thing. The contentions were laboriously shown to be hearsay. Hearsay was rejected as evidence.

The police case was that Geoff, frenziedly resisting arrest, had had to be carried in horizontally by the shoulders and ankles. He had been lashing out recklessly with his feet and had kicked a policeman in the groin so viciously that that officer had had to be hospitalized. The man struggling with his squirming shoulders had at this moment dropped him on the back of his head against a projection in the floor where a sliding partition had once slid in a groove. The pathologist was prepared to go as far as to assert that the injuries could be consonant with such a fall. He would not commit himself on how much force would actually be required to fracture the skull of a boy of Geoff's age and build. Much depended on the angle of impact. No one from Finsbury would believe that Geoff had simply been dropped. His head had been thrown down. That was the natural reaction, wasn't it, of a pig who saw that another pig had been hurt?

A modest-sized but for the most part idle crowd had gathered outside by the time the inquest was adjourned. They moved desultorily when the police required them to clear a passage. The Finsbury contingent came out in their scarves and rosettes and were shepherded to their minibus. There was verbal abuse but the police, watched by a surly inspector from across the street, were under strict orders to ignore what could break no bones.

Albert King and others, the Old Woman among them, drank themselves sentimental in a pub on the London side of the Chelmsford by-pass.

Cawthorne had had seniority over Kenworthy since they were both detective-sergeants. That was because in 1939

Kenworthy had gone into the army while Cawthorne—
loudly proclaiming that it was very much against his
will—had been claimed and reserved under some
internally invoked sub-para or other. But that was not
where the hostility between the two had started: it was
one of the little things that had helped. They had both
joined the force in the late 1930's, Kenworthy very much
against the wishes of his parents, who had fondly foreseen
a more academic or professional future for him. There
had been a hint of romanticism—or at least of melo-
drama—in his vision of what lay ahead of him.
Cawthorne had been on the same basic training
course—a big-mouthed cynic with an exalted idea of his
own main chance. It had been some source of quiet
satisfaction to the squad when an instructor had seen fit
to take Cawthorne on one side and talk to him about his
own image.

Their first plain-clothes experience had been on the
same night—as aides to CID on an exercise which needed
all the manpower that could be mustered. A sexual
hooligan had been molesting women on the South Bank:
mists creeping in off the oily-stinking river, a bronchial
ship's siren in the Pool. Men had been seconded from
wherever they could be found, paired with gymnastic
policewomen and deployed, hugging each other and the
shadows over a mile-long stretch, posing as courting
couples, waiting to pounce.

Young Kenworthy was not good at the amorous stuff.
He was at this time respectably courting Elspeth, then not
quite seventeen, and his partner for tonight was a hard-
bitten little vixen some three or four years senior to him in
the service, and disinclined to hide her opinion of his all-
round greenness. She was nearly a blonde, quite the
wrong size for him—and anxious to let him know from
the outset that he had better not expect too much realism
in this act. This was one of the first nights when the

London air-raid sirens were given a throaty practice airing, which added to the atmosphere the temptation to think of things to come. And a prowling DI came along early on, assessing the deployment of his front line.

'For Christ's sake—who are you? Which division have I won you from? Hold her at arm's length, man, if you can't stand the bloody sight of her. Look like it, man, for God's sake look like it. Show him how to set about it, Maureen.'

So they changed their stance. Even Maureen decided she might as well make the most of the evening. Kenworthy found himself getting quite to like her. Until later, over coffee at a wharfside gaff, she told him bluntly that he'd be better off sticking to Elspeth.

That wasn't the point. The man they were looking for was picked up elsewhere by others—but that wasn't the point, either. Cawthorne also took part in the exercise. Cawthorne always did seem to find his way on to anything for which Kenworthy had liked to think he had been specially selected. Cawthorne had been paired up with an Irish copperhead from Q Division, and from the way he talked about it afterwards, she'd be watching the calendar for a week or two to come. So Cawthorne said. It was Cawthorne's disregard for the girl's character that angered young Kenworthy. Kenworthy got up from the canteen table. Cawthorne followed him into the urinal.

'You're a bloody prig, aren't you, Kenworthy?'

Prig: it was one of those words so loaded that even to have it slung at you made you feel guilty—in 1939. And what the hell? He'd be what he wanted to be. If Cawthorne called that being a prig, God help him.

Later he was to learn of other differences between himself and Cawthorne—*Commander* Cawthorne, Cawthorne, Chairman of Natsecure.

There was, as Bransby-Lowndes had promised, a note

waiting for him in the outside office after lunch.
Whippletree's crossword editor would meet him in a bar
in Bloomsbury at seven that evening. No name, no
description, no recognition signals. Bransby-Lowndes
hadn't an operational clue. But Kenworthy didn't
anticipate difficulty. He knew the pub, a quiet one, and
he expected to be able to recognize the generic type of a
crossword editor. And Bransby-Lowndes must be allowed
his lucky dip into cloak and dagger fun.

Kenworthy walked up Kingsway from Aldwych. There
had been drizzle since tea-time and the pavements threw
up greasy reflections. Shopfronts, barred and grilled,
were lifeless with office equipment, philately, London
A-Z Guides. The pub was red plush and frosted windows.
He chose the private bar: his man would surely look in
them all. The only other drinker was a bronchitic,
checking place-odds in the margin of his evening paper.
Settled with a bitter in a corner, Kenworthy took an old
envelope from his wallet and began making notes about
another stage in the hierarchy. 1953—when he had first
made DI: where had they all been then? Cawthorne, he
knew, was already a Chief Inspector—south-west London
somewhere: New Malden or Raynes Park—bourgeois
burglaries. Dykes and Kershaw had been unknown
quantities to him in those days, chairborne names that
one saw in the lists—if one ever bothered to look: out on
the ground, one did not believe in the necessity for office-
wallahs. Bellamy, Richardson and Bragg had all been
DI's. He had never heard of Kershaw. Sam Tyrrell was
Detective-Superintendent, and there was a comet's tail of
stories about him that encouraged one to steer clear.

Kenworthy looked up when the door opened, but it was
only the punter's wife, handing him a key: she was going
out for the evening. Not a couple who had contributed
much to each other's well-being for some years.

Then a face showed at the window, someone standing

on tiptoes, looking over the frosted panel into one bar after another. The door opened again. Judith Pascoe came in.

She was wearing a see-through plastic raincoat over a lavender shirt with white jeans. She was quick to take off her head-scarf, shaking her hair free.

'Hullo.'

Surprise, surprise.

'Been swotting up holiday resorts in the British Museum?' he asked. 'What can I get you?'

White wine by the glass.

'Before we say anything else — there is something I must tell you. I've only just remembered. It had gone clear from my mind. While we were dining at the Festubert, Percy Mather and I, a man who had had too much to drink came by our table — '

She told him how a scrap of roll had fallen to the ground, how the drunk had picked it up, the head waiter replaced it.

'I just wondered. Could there have been sleight of hand? Some men are very clever.'

'What time was this?'

'We didn't sit down to eat till ten past eight.'

Kenworthy was doubtful. The first man to take a cab from there to Highgate had left at 7.45. That was vouched for in Mainfleet's boss's wife's log.

'I'm glad you remembered. Might come in useful. And are we both here with the same intent?'

'Seems so,' she said.

'Have you been contacting Bransby-Lowndes, then? Or did he contact you?'

'It was he who laid it on, was it?'

'At my request. We've just got to wait and see now, I suppose. To see who else blows in?'

'Are you really expecting him?'

'Men of that sort don't let people down, as a rule. I

expect he's stuck on the Underground somewhere.'

'Men of that sort? Has he suddenly sprouted reliability?'

'I've really no way of knowing how reliable he is.'

'Aren't we talking about Whippletree?'

'No. I'm talking about Whippletree's crossword editor.'

'I *am* Whippletree's crossword editor,' she said.

CHAPTER 15

It can take time to sort out cross-purposes of this sort. Judith's explanation would have been simpler and clearer if she had been in a position to think it out in advance. But she had been under the impression that she was coming here to meet Whippletree. Kenworthy understood in the end.

Like Whippletree, Judith Pascoe had made a precocious entry into crossword journalism. Her talent for subtle punning, her fluency with misleading parts of speech, made her a natural. Possibly the pleasure she got out of Early Norse was related to these talents. Like Whippletree she had contributed a weekly puzzle for years. It was only three years ago, following a death, that she had been asked to take over the co-ordinating role. She was glad to spare the few hours a week that it took.

'And Whippletree never suspected? Even though you must have had to correspond?'

'I signed myself Martin Grant. That was top editorial policy.'

'I'd have thought you were too strong a Women's Libber for that?'

'Never by direct assault. No woman who isn't a pragmatist will ever win her freedom. There are quite often letters from frustrated solvers—old men in club chairs who are no wiser when they've seen the answers.

Ancient dons plague me with obscure specialisms. It was decided not to add a woman's signature to the general state of discontent.'

A faint smile—but she was not in much of a smiling mood.

'You must have had a good deal of tongue-in-cheek fun in your first days in the Duchy.'

'It was—amusing.'

But not in retrospect, she implied.

'It's a pity he's spoiled it. That TV performance. What got into him?'

'I always hate to see a charming idyll dissolve on slender evidence,' Kenworthy said.

'Slender evidence? He was about to throw a brick through a window. And then he ran off. You call that slender? What was he even doing there?'

'Picking up half a brick. Running away when the law saw him. That's the sum total of the evidence. That's all we saw.'

'And you don't call that conclusive?'

'It says nothing about what he had in mind. You came here thinking to meet him. Doesn't that mean you were going to give him a chance to explain?'

'And to give him a piece of my mind. Do you know where to find him?'

'Don't you?' Kenworthy said.

She sighed.

'I'd dearly like to get hold of him for one reason alone. We do a massive puzzle for holidays. He was working on one for Christmas. It takes ages. I'd have to take a week's leave to do one myself.'

She opened the zip of a plastic document case and brought out a thin sheaf of papers.

'Peter Paul Whippletree has made a frightful mess of it—slapdash—alterations I can't read—even a spelling mistake in a vital place. One clue I can't understand—'

'And you've no idea where he is?'

'I know where he might be. He sometimes sends in his puzzles from a cottage in Suffolk. He spends weekends there, goes there for short leaves. We'd better ring and see if he's there.'

'Ringing will almost certainly ensure that he won't be. And incidentally—'

He looked at her uncertainly.

'Incidentally, if we turn up without notice, we mustn't be surprised—by anything—'

For once she was slow to pick up a hint.

'He's entitled to lead his own life,' she said at last coldly. 'All I want is some sense about this crossword. I couldn't face doing it from scratch.'

'So be it. Let's have a look at his country address.'

It seemed unnecessary to remind her that Whippletree might still think she had indeed slept with Percy Mather.

It was a long way to Kenworthy's car. He never drove in central London these days if he could avoid it. The Faculty had a standing order for garage space at the back of Victoria Street. They drove east and north-east, Forest Gate, Seven Kings, A 12, a seeming eternity of red traffic lights. It seemed a long time before they reached green fields—and then they weren't green, but an oceanic blackness, topped by a frantic stream of headlights. They stopped once for beer and a sandwich. For the last hour, neither of them had talked much.

'Where's it all going to end up?' she asked.

'With any luck, quietly nowhere. I mean that seriously. No one wants a shoot-out. I don't even care if bad men go unpunished—this time—as long as bad men are stopped from doing what they are doing.'

'You've known them a fairly long time, these bad men, haven't you?'

'Indeed I have.'

He remembered something and laughed, mostly to himself.

'It used to shock me, corruption in positions of trust. I used to say it would be a dangerous moment, if ever I failed to be shocked. The first case I really saw was in the army. I was a young NCO. We were supposed to be an elite. We were in Holland, autumn nineteen-forty-four, scouting for line-crossers in the hinterland of the Arnhem air-drop. Grey landscape, grey peasant faces, grey corpses up and down sodden fields. We had to draw stop-lines somewhere — a canal or a ditch. Anybody crossing had to account for himself. Sometimes we had to split a man's fields, even his livestock — those that hadn't trodden on mines, or got mixed up in artillery fire. We improvised a pass system. Priests, teachers, burgomasters helped us to check *bona fides*. What I am coming to is this: an old smallholder needed a pass to feed his pig. One of our patrols — he'd been an Oxford don two years previously — was charging him a chicken every time he crossed.'

'So what did you do about it?'

'Had roast chicken instead of tinned M and V for supper.'

The landlord was calling last orders. Kenworthy checked his watch.

'I still think it was bad. And it shook me, what I saw in the Met: some parts of the Met. And they're still winning.'

'It's had plenty of publicity.'

'The more obvious abuses have. Usually it was men who had to run with the hares to get information — and took a cut for keeping their eyes shut. Now and then in order to survive they had to pull in someone who thought he'd bought himself protection. That caused resentment. Led to super-grasses. But there were worse practices — at least, I thought they were. Because these were not being worked by the middle ranks. They were the perks of the top people — the people who do your crosswords.'

She was watching him intently, listening intently; he was talking intently. She had not known him long enough to hear him talk like this before.

'You've heard of Superintendents and at least one Commander going under. There were Superintendents and Commanders among this lot—but that wasn't all. There were also some of the big noises from behind the scenes: high Civil Servants. You'd think you had to be out in the field, to be where the lucre was—but some men will always find a way. There were bad men living off other bad men, twice removed. It had to be a big job—an extravagant robbery, a wage-snatch, a wholesale drug-haul, an illegal immigrant-run on the grand scale, a country-wide insurance fiddle. A Chief Super in the field might have been working on it for months. I know: I've been in that position. Your papers would go on. After a few more months they'd go on again, thousands of filed, bound documents, over to the DPP. Only to be chucked out, because the Attorney-General doesn't care to back losing cases. And why were they losing cases? Because between the investigating Chief Super and the DPP's staff, something had happened to the file. A vital stage in the case might have been expressed differently, could be missing altogether. The thing had been edited. It was a defective case that had gone forward. Even an exhibit of concrete evidence has been known to be suddenly unaccounted for. I have known an investigating officer accused of never having passing it forward in the first place. Sometimes you did not even know why your case had been chucked out. It was vaguely blamed on the DPP, and the general belief was put round that he was a bit of an ass. That was how a man called Cawthorne sold protection to men who were not even his clients—working through linkmen like Bragg and Bellamy. Those were just a few of the advantages that accrued from operating L(Y) Branch. But I don't want to bore you with details.'

'Those are the Egham names.'

'Yes. And wouldn't it be nice to see them queuing to slop out? Learning to sew prison uniforms? Intriguing for shreds of contraband tobacco? But I tell you, Judith, I don't care whether it comes to that or not. Cawthorne's come-uppance can wait. What matters to me is to see Natsecure quietly wound up. Are we ready for the road?'

They by-passed towns that were already beginning to think of bed. Allotments and forecourts and Garden Centres had been deserted by humanity. They left the arterial road and plunged into pastoral Suffolk. Self-sufficient little market towns slumbered round Noddyland branches of the High Street Banks. It was rising midnight when they drew into Whippletree's village: houses not numbered, very few of them named — and no lane with a sign to match the address that Judith had for Whippletree. Fortunately the publican at the Loaves and Fishes looked on the licensing laws as a personal challenge, and it was possible through the window to attract the attention of one of the half-dozen still in the public bar.

Winter Cottage was several bramble-corners removed from the sight of any other village habitation, down a flint and dust road that was here beginning a sharp descent. As they got out of the car, Kenworthy slamming the door as hard as he could, they could hear the close sibilance of a beach. A red MG, a buff's car, was parked sideways on in the gateway of an orchard. Kenworthy parked blocking the approach from either direction. A very pale light appeared behind the curtain of an upstairs window. The pane opened twenty degrees wider than it already was, and a voice shouted down.

'Who is it? What do you want?'

'Kenworthy. And your crossword editor. You're in trouble with 17 Across and 4 Down.'

'Half a minute.'

Whippletree, his hair pillow-ruffled, a Marks and Spencer's dressing-gown over creased pyjamas, let them in through a lean-to scullery. He was carrying a candle, folded a spill to light an oil-lamp on the table of his living-room. There was a pump by the rotting wooden draining-board by the sink. It seemed likely that the cottage was totally lacking in outside services. But Whippletree had made his mark on it. It was improbable that he was an apostle of the good life; what was likely to appeal to him about the primitive was that it was unbothered, undemanding. His books ranged from Penguin greenback to Böll and Dürrenmatt in the original. He seemed specially fond of Turgenev. Currently lying on chair-arms were Dixon's *Psychology of Military Incompetence* and Montaigne's *Essais* in the sixteenth-century text. His contract with the world beyond the end of his lane was a transistor radio that looked as if a frying-pan spattered it regularly.

He blinked at Judith Pascoe.

'I thought you said—'

She unzipped her case and cast the draft of his giant crossword down on his table.

'Not a very clever ploy,' he said, obviously putting it all down to Kenworthy.

'There are one or two things you owe it to us to tell us,' Kenworthy said.

'I don't want to know any more about any of it.'

There was a half-finished packet of king-sized filter-tips on his table. Whippletree did not smoke. Kenworthy had noticed lipstick on a cup-rim on the draining-board. He did not know whether Judith had seen it. Judith picked up the puzzle again.

'At least you'll want to know about this—before you get the editor's regrets. I'd hate to do that to you.'

He was still not ready to believe.

'Martin Grant. The very long arm of coincidence. And

how moronic can you get? What's this "A teetotal feat for taking silk?" '

'Tafetta!'

'Two F's and one T.'

'Oh Christ! That's what comes of travelling without Chambers's.'

'It also invalidates 6 Down. And your blunderbuss 1 Across is in jeopardy. "Animal, vegetable and mineral" is rather good. It's going to hold a lot of people up.'

'Do you know how long this bloody well took me?'

'Nearly as long as it's going to take to put right. Mind you, I think I can see a way round things.'

There were sounds of someone getting out of bed in the room above them. Judith gave no sign that she had heard.

'Coffee? Something stronger? I'll give my mind to this in a minute. I'm still a little off-true. There are explanations pending.' He addressed himself to Kenworthy. 'But I'm still having no more to do with your side of the thing.'

'You might listen to a little about it. Even if only for the sake of what we're trying to avert.'

'Why avert it? Why put it off till next month? It's going to happen sooner or later. I've lost interest.'

'Which side were you interested in, anyway?' Kenworthy asked him.

'Do you ask? The side that can go and stew, as far as I am concerned.'

Footsteps began to come down creaking stairs, which were shut off from the living-room by a latched door.

'You've regressed, Whippletree,' Kenworthy said. 'Why, for God's sake?'

Mentally, emotionally, spiritually, Whippletree did seem to be at the bottom of a gulf. But Kenworthy gave the impression of a man whose well of patience was truly inexhaustible. The latched door opened and a girl stepped through it. She was wearing a pink nylon

nightdress that reached to about eight inches above her
knees, its yoke catastrophically too wide for her shoulders.
She stood about five feet, an artificial and dishevelled
blonde. Her mouth was slack, her lips full, red and moist.

'Deirdre?'

'Pass me my ciggies, Pete.'

The vowel-sounds of the East End of London seemed to
have got themselves caught up into the intonational
melody of Suffolk. Whippletree reached for the packet
and slid it back to where she could reach it. There were
no introductions. She went back upstairs without saying
more.

'Here beginneth—' Whippletree said. 'I suppose I am
about to hear the First Lesson. But I warn you—I've
heard it all before—from some accredited Grand Masters
of the genre.'

'I'm not in a preaching mood,' Kenworthy said. 'I don't
think either of us is.'

He did not look at Judith for support—nor indeed to
see what facial expression she was wearing.

'You're in a strong position to give us help that we
need, Whippletree. I might have expected you to be
mixed-up about it.'

'It isn't my mix-up that's put English society where it
is,' Whippletree said.

'No? We shall just have to manage without you, then.
All because you were once caned—hurt—for having a
name like Whippletree. Well, I could tell you a story
about cutting off my nose to spite my face, because I was
caned—hurt—for a damned sight less. In fact, by
comparison, having a name like Whippletree seems to be
a bloody good reason for flaying the skin off a man's arse.'

Whippletree looked at him blankly.

'Back in nineteen-thirty-five. I was in my fifth year at
Grammar School. The year we did the old School
Cert—Matriculation. We had an inadequate old bugger

called Rooke who came to our classroom when the timetable said History. He was neurotic, obsessed with his own image and precedence, always suspecting he was under attack. Which, of course, he was. You can't expect a class of sixteen-year-olds not to spot the vulnerability of a Charlie like that. They made life hell for him. Then he'd go at us like a battering-ram: thunderbolt reprisals against trivialities. Now I was by temperament and upbringing a fairly submissive type. The exams mattered to me. I must even have still been clinging to the belief that I was learning History from Rooke. One particular lesson turned into a near-mutiny. I had had nothing to do with it. I'm not trying to make out I was a saint — I'm just telling it as it was. But Rooke happened to look at me at the worst possible moment. I must have let my face go — I can't describe how I was looking at him — it must have been with a mixture of pity and disgust. I could see right through him. I was bored. I was wishing he'd get on with the lesson. And whatever he saw in my eyes punctured him. He interpreted it as dumb insolence — and named me to the headmaster as one of the chief insubordinates.'

The girl upstairs must be turning over in bed. It sounded as if one of its legs was about to come through the floor.

'The headmaster thrashed me — the first and only time. They sometimes describe pain as exquisite. That just about says it. Then he put his cane away ceremoniously and kept me standing.

' "Now I know, Kenworthy, you're not the sort of boy to make a fuss about a thing like this."

'He knew, and he knew that I knew, that I had been sacrificed to placate the establishment. It was his job to support Rooke. The system demanded it. That's why I wouldn't stay at school after the end of that year. That's why I cut all chance of higher education from under myself. That's what took me into the Met as soon as I was old enough. That's why I haven't forgiven the system yet. Because in my case the system has repeated itself more than once. And that's how I know something of what's going on in your mind, young Whippletree.'

'There are other things too, in my case,' Whippletree said.

'Likewise. But let's now start talking about present and future.'

Whippletree's blankness had now developed into a sort of passive expectancy.

'You know you were on television?'

'I did wonder.'

'The wonder is that you weren't spotted by more of your friends. Judith and I saw you. You were about to heave a brick. Then you ran away from a policeman.'

'He wasn't a policeman.'

'Oh?'

'He was Natsecure. He had his back to the camera, hadn't he? I'd watched the same man stand by while a gang of three was making hay of a video display. But the moment my arm was crooked in the direction of a Regency wine-store, he was after me with his night-stick. He did what I thought he'd do. I wanted to find out for myself.'

Whippletree seemed to have decided to make himself explicit, at least as far as this episode was concerned.

'When I was doing that thing about football hooligans, I got copy-notes from police forces about incidents in their areas. I was surprised about how much cooperation I did get. That sort of thing can happen now and then, when you're a government department: and when all you're asking for basically is a shower of paper. Some police authorities were more informative than others. One area even listed premises that were damaged: card shops, TV rentals, fancy stationers. It was only in an idle moment that I got to thinking about the omissions—the places that were not damaged. I can't say all off-licences escaped: accidents will happen. But never was a Regency attacked, and Regency is a big chain.'

'Do you put that down to protection—or discipline?' Kenworthy asked.

'A little of both, I think—but discipline wasn't too hot. These light commandos, on the Parkeston pattern, would come in from a distance, led by someone who wasn't in evidence while the actual scrap was on. They are comparatively new to the scene. And all sorts of things suggest that the hooligans do as they're told, some of the time.'

'I should like to read this thing of yours about football thugs,' Kenworthy said.

'It was too heavily cut by the top corridor. Any fool can talk about keeping rivals apart, searching for flick-knives, closing the pubs. All that was left in. And I didn't exactly blame it all on the decline of the English Sunday School, but it does all boil down to an outlook. And outlooks can be nourished. But no government likes to be reminded gratuitously of what it's not doing for education—'

The stairs again, an uneven tread. One could almost picture where the girl was standing for a second to let a flickering candle-flame pick itself up. Whippletree looked apathetically resigned to a fresh appearance by Deirdre. She came through the door again with one of his very old tweed jackets hanging loosely about her shoulders, the frayed cuffs swinging unoccupied. It was a small room, and everybody had to move for her to walk purposefully over to the scullery door. She stood by it with her hand on the latch, looking at Whippletree with sullen eyes.

'Well? I'm not going out there on my tod.'

Whippletree stood up, compelled to turn his resignation into practice. He picked up a red plastic torch from a shelf and opened the door to accompany her into the night. The hiss of distant surf reached into the room while the back door was open. Kenworthy and Judith looked at each other.

'Not his proudest moment,' Kenworthy said.

Judith was resting her face against her fingers, her eyes wandering idly over Whippletree's books and etchings — yet she did not appear to be taking in what she saw. There were aspects of this encounter that had not yet fully developed inside her.

'Where do you think they found each other?' she asked.

'He must occasionally find himself at a loose end.'

'She is the original loose end.'

There were sounds of returning feet on the brick path outside, of twigs being caught by sleeves. Deirdre preceded Whippletree into the room, nodded affably at Judith and went straight back upstairs.

'Even if you don't want to play much part in events,' Kenworthy said, 'there are one or two essentials that I wish you'd give your mind to. The question of certain files, for example.'

'Files?'

'You brought with you from the Duchy some documents. Their absence is upsetting our friend Burton's economy.'

Whippletree's reaction was remarkable. For some reason the mention of files sent him into a flying rage.

'Why doesn't somebody think of something new? The oldest one in the book. I shall write a dissertation one of these days: files I have been blamed for losing. It's a marvellous device, you know. It doesn't just kill two birds with one stone: it goes through a bloody flock like a cheese through skittles. You get rid of something that's likely to sink you, and somebody else gets it in the neck into the bargain. Do you know, I was once accused of making away with a file on *Indications of evidence of land-tenure in Lincolnshire folk-songs.*'

Kenworthy waited until he had subsided.

'No files?' he then said quietly.

'No files.'

'But I expect you'll know what files it is that Burton has in mind?'

'That must be obvious. The one that started all the trouble. The one that fell into Percy's hands—in the intermediate stages of setting up the Egham lark. Some clerk had clipped a couple of sheets of flimsy in that weren't meant to be there. Percy was so upset that he talked to me about it—well, he *did* talk to me sometimes—'

'Did he show them to you?'

'I glanced at it. He did not give me long enough. I could not quote any detail. It was the sort of thing you'd have to study. In fact there was a lot about it I didn't understand at all. What's come to me since is that it was a template for battle: the phases of disposition—first and second waves, police withdrawals and regroupings—that sort of thing.'

'Did it say *where* this was going to happen?'

'Not to my knowledge. I certainly did not see that. I did not give enough attention to it. It was a matter of principle never to look as if you were taking anything seriously in the Duchy.'

'Even when Percy was seriously het up about it?'

'Especially when Percy was seriously het up about it!'

'And what happened to this file?'

'Percy said he was going to take it to show Burton. Oh—I can't say I blame him for that. Burton and I wouldn't opt to spend a long weekend together in a Welsh mountain chalet. But if you were mad enough to take the Duchy seriously and wanted action, there was only Burton you could go to.'

'Talk to me about Burton.'

'Well—once you knew you were stuck with the insanity of the Duchy, there were various illusions you could shelter behind. Burton's illusion was that he could replace it all by some greater insanity of his own.'

That seemed to dispose of Burton. Kenworthy waited, but nothing else was forthcoming.

'You know, Whippletree, you disappoint me. If one turns your handle, one lives in hope that more than one tune will come out. You can tell us more about Burton than that. Obviously, like everyone except yourself, he is misguided. But isn't he honestly misguided?'

'It depends what you mean by honesty. If you mean the tactics of everyday manipulation—'

'You know very well what I do mean.'

'I'd describe him as a clinical case of abortive integrity.'

'I don't want to put ideas into your head, but might he have known about the original Egham intent all along—before Mather went to him? Might he in fact not have been one of its architects? Might he not have scrubbed it out as smartly as he did in order to dissociate himself from it?'

'No. Not Burton. I'll stake what reputation I have on that.'

But Whippletree's face suggested that he was giving this further thought.

'There's one thing that worries me, though. In my book they killed Percy. So why haven't they killed Burton?'

'Yet.'

It seemed a long stretch from the littered, bachelor-scruffy, barely converted East Anglian hovel to cool talk about strategic assassination.

'So tell us more about him,' Kenworthy urged.

'I don't know more about him. There *isn't* any more about him.'

'Don't be silly, man. His wife, his family, his interests? Where does he go for his holidays? Did you know he feeds the pigeons on his window-ledge?'

'I don't know anything at all about his private

personality. It's always struck me as a revolting thought that he should have one.'

'I just wonder if that might be a possible weakness in your school of human analysis. Tell me something about Bessemer, then. And don't say he thinks he's a teapot. What's his trouble?'

'He sees every point of view,' Whippletree said. 'And he's totally incapable of choices between them. In office life, he was for ever consulting. One wishes other people sometimes would—but Bessemer went on asking second opinions for ever. If you wanted things done your way, you made sure you were the last one to plague him. Another honest man. In practice, of course, in Bessemer's day, everyone went their own way. And in the general run, Bessemer got nothing worse out of it than permanent misery. But if a real conflict came up—if it came to reconciling incompatibles—then Bessemer went under. That was how he came to the Duchy. He'd been at DHSS: case-work officer, and had had a nervous breakdown: blamed himself for somebody's suicide.'

'And at the Duchy?'

'Oh, he'd got over it by the time they transferred him. I've cracked jokes with Bill Bessemer.'

'I mean—why did he break down in III (Populace)?'

'That's a mystery. I don't know that there was ever a single trigger. We certainly didn't think there was—but then, we didn't think there had to be. We knew his history. We knew he had moody days. We used to make bets on how many times we could get him to change his mind at a section meeting. There came a time when he seemed less accessible than usual—then not accessible at all. As we did not need him, we did not bother him. Then he was off sick, and he didn't come back. Then we heard—'

'And when was this?'

Whippletree thought hard.

'Two or three months before you came, Judith.'

'In other words, after the ground-work for Egham had started?'

'Yes—it must have been.'

'So Bessemer had some of the handling of it.'

'I suppose he had. I apologize if I sound as if I don't care. None of us could pose as experts as to what's going on in an Assistant Secretary's mind. We're apt to assume that most of the time nothing is.'

Judith came into the dialogue, factually and objectively.

'Have you heard that III (Populace) has been decimated since you left?'

She told him who had been transferred and who remained.

'Any comment?'

'I don't think so. One assumes it's only a temporary measure. A spasm. A Burtonism.'

'Anyone you think Burton may have moved for ulterior motives?'

'Not at first impact.'

'Anyone who was particularly active at plaguing Bessemer?'

'We didn't really plague Bessemer. We only played with him.'

Judith withdrew. Kenworthy took over again.

'While we are talking personalities—and I'm not interested in caricatures—you people do seem to treat each other as cartoon profiles—'

But he stopped. The stairs were creaking again. There was no point in starting on anyone else if Deirdre was going to walk across the scene again. She opened the door and looked only at Whippletree.

'Are you going to be long?'

It was a sad, suffering drawl. Whippletree got up, went to her, turned her through 180 degrees, smacked her bottom amicably through the gossamer nightdress and propelled her up the first two treads. He closed the door behind her and went back to his chair.

'Suffolk's all right if you know you're going back to London the day after tomorrow. For longer stays, the resources are limited.'

No one took him up on that.

'Sir Henry?' Kenworthy asked. 'And don't tell me he's lazy. Don't mention Huguenot silver.'

'Certainly not King Stork,' Whippletree answered. 'King Flotsam's about as far as I would go. We don't even know if he's a log.'

'I had a little to do with him the other day,' Kenworthy said. 'And he did not strike me as incapable.'

'Ah! There I can see the Duchy entering into your soul. Once you have met some of our leading lights, you can even find praise for Sir Henry. I'm sorry again. What you call my school of human analysis breaks down once more. Sir Henry tries to memorize one personal fact to attach to every face he meets about the building. He'll ask one how his digestion is, another about his cacti. In my case he knows that my father and uncle were army men. This is known as winning friends without being influenced by them.'

'Well—we'll try one more—just to see if you know anything about anybody. Ted Thompson?'

'Ah!'

Whippletree's face showed some influx of light for the first time.

'A womanizer.'

Judith's eyebrows climbed an inch or two.

'Is he really?'

'Oh—on a generous scale. Starting with the one he married. A German. A legacy of his National Service—or perhaps we should regard her as part of his gratuity. Paper and pulp. Heiress—since her brothers gave their

blood for the Fatherland. Mind you, they lost a lot of
growing timber to the DDR and Poland—but Marshall
Aid had to put somebody back on their feet to meet the
demand for newsprint. A good-looker too, though mind
you, she's gone the way of the Hausfrau. A capacious
child-bearing pelvis and a forehead you could print
banner headlines on. And you'd have to use your full
share of imagination to remember that she was once a
classical Aryan blonde. The thing is, she keeps old Ted on
a calculated leash. And she knows what she's at: not so
tight that it chafes—but when she gives it one of her little
tugs, he knows all about it. The sort of tug he'll
remember till next time.'

In contrast to a few minutes ago, he was talking with
the fluency of an entertainer who has come to a happy
passage in his act. Kenworthy prodded him with teasing
irony, but with no intention to puncture.

'You know all this, do you?'

'Common knowledge.'

'What are his diversions, then? How does he divert
himself until he feels a tug?'

Whippletree shrugged his shoulders.

'He can't pass a girl on a corridor without—'

'Yes, yes. That's merely his nuisance value. And I am
sure there are girls who know when and where to plant
themselves along the corridor walls. What about his wider
excursions? I'm sure they haven't escaped the attentions
of III (Populace).'

But pressed in this fashion, Whippletree was not the
fount of information that he gave out to be. It was
tempting to write him off as a mere gossip.

'Old Ted knows better than to give key facts away,' he
said.

A few minutes after that, Kenworthy was getting them
to their feet, declining one for the road.

'You won't be coming back to London in the near

future, then? You've slipped the noose of the Duchy for good?'

Whippletree looked plainly uncertain.

'I daren't come back to London. Surely you see that. Whoever did for Percy must assume that I was in Percy's pocket. We did talk to each other quite a lot, as a matter of fact.'

He looked at Judith as if he felt that he ought to apologize to her for that.

'They're bound to assume that I knew as much as Percy knew—which isn't true. For the same reason, since you two have almost certainly been observed, I can't stay here, either. I don't know where I shall go; or even how long my meagre capital will last.'

He picked up the monster crossword and looked at it fleetingly.

'I'll see what I can do with this. I'll send you an accommodation address—when I've got one. In the meanwhile, I'll submit these as usual—unless, that is, I'm ruled out—?'

He looked at her with the melancholy query.

'We won't mix business with displeasure,' she said. 'Whatever you send, I'll consider on its merit.'

And if she had meant that to sound icy, she had underestimated her capacity to freeze. Kenworthy shot her a glance of admiration. They went out into the lane towards his car.

'One moment—'

He took a few steps down the slope so that he could look through a gap in low cliffs down on to a beach. The creaming white of the tide-line was just visible through the thinly clouded night. As they drove back up past Winter Cottage, a feeble light was still to be seen behind the curtains of an upper window. Judith's eyes were turned to the other side of the car.

CHAPTER 16

Country lanes and sleeping Suffolk towns, with their street-lights—where they had any—switched off. They came back to the arterial road, and as they pulled away from the access roundabout, Kenworthy depressed his right foot.

Judith was disinclined to talk. They had not discussed their impressions of the conversation in the cottage, had attempted no analysis. Judith's mind, involuntarily and insistently, kept returning to another cottage—the one in the Fens: the man-channelled river and the grid of rush-fringed dykes. She was not thinking of her last visit there, but of her very first: of Ian MacIntyre looking like a huggable young bear in his casual morning machismo. He sat out on the fen, marking Tripos scripts. That was the reason his wife accepted for his needing solitude. Judith did minimal housewifely chores and made it look as if she were cross-referencing texts for her thesis. Time drifted by and what she deluded herself was *thought*.

Last night had been the first night. She was no angel—now. And the thought that she was no angel brought her an odd sort of liberating pleasure: almost a comfort, for an academic.

She was no angel. Therefore she had sacrificed the right to demand angelic conduct from others. She had known that that was how she would have to look on life henceforward. But Ian MacIntyre was no swap for Deirdre; that was what was rankling.

The outskirts of London began to claim them. Rows of predictable shops were set back along service-roads, some of their windows pointlessly lit up all night. Kenworthy spoke out of the blue.

'I don't know where he found her—but I doubt very much if he's committed.'

He must be a mind-reader—and there was nothing very clever or surprising about that.

Suburban Broadways gave way to grimier walls—to older, muckier premises. And there was a new element, which she was sure had sprung up since yesterday evening. On end-walls, on hoardings, painted across pavement setts was a slogan:

GEOFF KING—BLOOD FOR BLOOD.

Hewitson waited for Kenworthy to finish reading the pathologist's report.

'Is anybody in this country, in any walk of life, doing an honest job of work nowadays?'

'You certainly can't rely on it. Could you ever?'

'I've known pathologists in my time who would never have missed a trick—even on a Saturday afternoon.'

No one doubted that Percy Mather had died of cardiac failure due to myocardial infarction. It was a forgivable assumption, even before the exploratory knife had entered the cadaver. And what had been expected had been found. Nor, on paper, had the rest of the examination been neglected. Every section of the official form had been filled in. Percy Mather's last meal had been recorded, though not perhaps in the same language as on the menu. Grilled sole with its garnishing, French beans and *Bleu de Bresse*.

But that had been reckoned enough. What had been listed were the bits that had not been digested. There was no analysis of juices, no search for noxious substances—because there had so obviously been no need for that: which amounted to professional negligence of a disgraceful if understandable order. Especially since cremation had now settled Mather's dyspepsia, real or induced.

'Mind you,' Hewitson said. 'I don't see that there need have been any noxious substance. There's evidence that he was suffering from nausea. The taxi-driver saw it, the Pascoe girl saw it, Mather complained of it himself.'

Hewitson was a modern policeman: that is to say, an advanced technician, backed by unmistakable hints of flair—and the ability to assimilate his ever-growing experience. He was also prepared to peg away at unpromising routines.

'I don't see that we need a noxious substance. I've asked the medics, and a man might not be feeling up to much in the run-up to a coronary.'

'But he had to be made to feel ill,' Kenworthy said. 'Don't you see that? It had to be certain that Judith Pascoe would take him into her flat. It had to be certain that she would go out for the doctor. Why else was it necessary to tamper with her phone?'

'If your theory is correct. Look, Simon, I know you've got it worked out. A man went out to Highgate by taxi as soon as the pair were settled down to their meal at the Festubert. Another man was waiting in Bishopwood Road for the couple to arrive there. Judith Pascoe went for her doctor. Her doctor says so. We know that the semen on the sheet was not Mather's. We also know—because I've had that checked too, now, that the pyjamas were not Mather's, either. So I'd like to accept your theory—if only because I know of no other that fits. But there's a snag.'

They were in Hewitson's office. Hewitson had asked Kenworthy to call.

'It's not a criminal planner's way of setting about it. It depends on too many felicitous events, an interlocking of too many things over which a man has no control. Even the death at the end of it seems to have been a massive stroke of luck. Is that how you'd plan a murder?'

'I'd not have relied on it to the exclusion of every-thing else, but it could have been my number one plan—because it's such a damned good one if it works. But I'd certainly have backed it up with alternatives. After all, it needn't even have succeeded on the Saturday night—though you can see the murderer's point of view in wanting Mather out of the way sooner rather than later.'

'All right, let's say there were alternative plans. So there had to be alternative teams—no problem, if as big a machine as Natsecure is involved. The one common point from which they'd all have to start is this: it had to be known that Mather was taking the girl out to dinner, and where. Do you agree?'

'I do.'

Hewitson did not get excited. This was not a personal competition.

'I've not got unlimited time, but they're being generous with me. They're not cribbing when I ask for men—and insist on good ones. So for a couple of days, I'm going to follow up as many plans as I can find for the murderer. I'm prepared to play-act as many schemes, setting out from the Festubert, as seem to be feasible. Now, give your mind to it, Simon. From the time when they went for their coats at the restaurant, how many courses of action did Mather and Judith Pascoe have? Let's not be too fanciful. They were both feeling tired, one was old, and feeling one degree under. They'd hardly think of a nightclub.'

'Not either one's scene, anyway.'

'We'll say not, for the moment. Miss Pascoe, knowing Mather to be ill, might have insisted on getting Mather to his home first.'

'He'd have regarded that as ungentlemanly.'

'That depends partly on how ill he felt. And Miss Pascoe might have been forceful. I'm going to follow that up, anyway—because your murderer would. Then they could have gone their separate ways.'

'Discourteous.'

'But it could have played hell with mice and men if they had. Therefore the murderer would have considered it.'

There was more than a threshold of joy in working with Hewitson: he got on.

Kenworthy was always frightened by hospitals for the mentally sick. There must come a time when regular visitors to such places take the ethos for granted, otherwise they could not continue to be visitors. One is always afraid of being accosted by someone who is pushing an unreasoned conviction to the point of violence, but this was not where the obscenity lay for Kenworthy. One might be afraid of a sick face, of terrified eyes, of sexual gluttony oozing from a revolting body. But the real fear was the thought of what it would be like to have to live a communal life in dormitories or dayrooms like these.

Behind the lee of a boiler-house, a group of men in trousers that did not match jackets, and in waistcoats that matched neither, were leaning against the brickwork and squabbling through twisted teeth. These were the mentally retarded, the Mongols, the cretins, whatever, the ineducable, the men of forty with the brains of six-year-olds. They were in a different class from Bessemer, but they lived here too.

Kenworthy had hardly hoped to be allowed to see Bessemer, but it would have been the nadir of negligence not to have made an attempt. He did not expect to get past the psychiatrist. In eventual fact, he lost hope of even reaching that barrier.

The psychiatrist was a man called Herzfeld, a Hungarian. He had a facial tic which he had assimilated into his conversational style, using it like a stab of unanswerable rhetorical question between his staccato statements of authority. One felt that if ever a man was due for a change of company, he was. He fired at Kenworthy through the loopholes in his professional stockade. Was he to be expected to discuss the confidences of a patient? Certainly there could be no question whatsoever of Kenworthy's even being allowed a sight of the man. Bessemer had only to catch a hint that an outsider was interested in him for six weeks' therapy to be undone. Kenworthy was mild and submissive, even apologized for being here. But did not Dr Herzfeld think that if he discussed Bessmer's case, he might learn something that would help him to help his patient?

'Help him? There's only one help we can hope to give him at present—to put and maintain him in a condition where he does not have to make a decision. Whether there will ever come a time when he will ever again be able to stand at any mental crossroads without panic is a moot point.'

Dr Herzfeld's eyes looked diagonally past Kenworthy's and the flesh over his right cheek-bone was caught up in two ferocious twitches, a challenge to Kenworthy to deny clinical expertise. Was not the question rather, Kenworthy asked, whether Bessemer ever had been capable of selecting between (a) and (b)?

Herzfeld got up and looked out of his window, overlooking the gravelled drive that led from the residential and treatment barracks to the somehow more civilized windows of the administrative block. The official visiting hour had finished a few minutes ago and a long line of the relatively sane were shuffling through the gravel towards the car park. Herzfeld beckoned to Kenworthy to come and see.

'Bessemer's wife and daughter.'

Mrs Bessemer—it was hard not to think of her as a widow—was a well-dressed middle-aged woman whose permanent wave suggested that she still wanted to belong to the 1940's. She had been crying, and the rims of her eyes must have been smarting. Even now she had to stand and bring a laced twist of handkerchief out of her handbag. The daughter was in her late married twenties, in a hip-length imitation leopardskin coat and spike-heeled knee-boots. She stood, half turned, a yard and a half in front of her mother while she dabbed her eyes, her impatience to be away from these precincts communicating itself even at this distance, as if she had to be physically out of the grounds before she could shake them from her memory.

'They know that to have him home again would be worse than having him here,' Herzfeld said. 'But he is progressing. When he first came here, even tomorrow's diet-sheet was a trauma. He'd spend the whole afternoon fretting whether he'd made the right choice for the next morning's breakfast. He'd go down to the dietician's office to try to make a change, then hover outside the door and not dare to knock on it. And you want to go and remind him of the Duchy of Axholme!'

'I can see that that would serve no useful purpose.'

'You would recall to his mind the existence of two men called Burton and Thompson. Have you met them? I've only heard of them.'

'I've come across them briefly.'

'I tell myself, as I tell him, they aren't ogres at all. But to him they are worse than terrors. They are symbols of the two ways he is being pulled. If we could only find out what the division is—'

Kenworthy saw no point in not believing that Herzfeld knew what he was talking about.

There was a rash of slogans as Kenworthy drove back to central London. GEOFF KING—BLOOD FOR BLOOD under the coping stones of railway arches; GEOFF KING—MURDERED, in red aerosol where an estate-developer's poster had been torn away from the woodwork. The slogan-writers had moved in two directions. There was optimistic invention, none of it very clever or memorable: KING OF THE BROKEN CROWN—FASCIST ASSASSINS.

Someone else had gone for simplicity, if not for immediate logic. His inspiration was destined to become the battle-cry of the campaign: KING GEOFF RULES—OK.

And there was another thing, that had about it some of the unaccountability of a minor miracle. In places where unoccupied men gathered—on the corner-lots of demolitions, on the pavements outside betting-shops, Kenworthy spotted here and there a scarf in orange and green: the so-called Alpine green and the dull, dark orange of the Finsbury colours. He saw it in places surely far removed from any loyalty to Finsbury—Edmonton, Walthamstow, Leyton.

It made him wonder whether someone—fanatical family knitters apart—was organizing a supply of Finsbury scarves.

Judith Pascoe needed work. She needed a surfeit, a welter of it, that would dispose of time and the opportunities time gave for uncreative thought. It was not only the memory of Whippletree's tart in her translucent nylon. There was also Whippletree's abject failure to come to any kind of manly grip with the pending disaster. She did not really know what Whippletree could be expected to do about it. What nauseated her was the emetic certainty of his determination to do nothing, to refuse to align himself with corporate decency, even at this stage. And she felt sure of one thing: that he knew something; something that he ought to have rushed to share with Kenworthy. But if Whippletree were to try to return here, if for some internal tactic the powers-that-be were to take him in again, she would refuse to have him in her section.

She would make a resignation issue out of that, if necessary. She was having no difficulty in making herself hate Whippletree.

The only work on her desk—the only pastime that Burton would allow her—was the changing taste of visitors to seaside towns. She had already sketched out a trial plan of action, had filled her head with the prose of the introductory paragraphs. That would have to be a historical survey: the Prince Regent, piers and bathing-machines. Scenic railways, aquaria and Butlin's: her mind was carried back to holidays she had had as a girl. Clacton and Littlehampton. What her parents had been doing, of course, was trying to recapture their own youth.

She sent for the lonely remainder of her Study Group and allocated aspects to them: including statistics, where they could be got at. A table of figures every few pages made it look scientific. The demand for gambling: people who played bingo five nights a week at home were dying to play all day on holiday. Fruit machines. Casinos. The cinema was dead: but were Punch and Judy? What about mapping out rock-pool foreshores as nature trails? Self-catering versus the boarding-house? And how ought the English pub to cater for children?

The project was not without its possibilities; nor, given a sensible programme, was the Duchy. By the time she had scribbled a thousand words about the Victorians' discovery of their coast, half the morning was pleasantly consumed. Then the messenger came with his mid-morning armful of buff envelopes, which included mail from the world outside. She saw Whippletree's Chancery hand on a letter postmarked Epworth, Lincs. What the devil was he doing up there? Beginning to take an interest in the Isle of Axholme at last?

She laid it to one side, was tempted to throw it unopened into her wastepaper-basket, went conscientiously through everything official before she picked it up again. There were official circulars about not wasting stationery, and something from Iliffe about the staff shutting windows before they went off duty.

Then she slit open Whippletree's envelope—a frustrating job, because he had gone to such lengths with Sellotape. There was no covering letter. On top was the amended version of his Jumbo crossword, and a quick look in the crucial places was enough to assure that he had made a job of it this time. So one at least of life's difficulties was cleared. But she staunchly prevented herself from feeling any sense of gratitude to Whippletree for that. That was precisely what he was trying to work her round to, and she was damned if she was going to fall for it.

But underneath the outsize square and its clues there was another enclosure, indeed another crossword. But this one was different from the normal mode of submission. The accepted thing was for him to send two copies each of the blank squares. Here there were only one copy each of the clues and the puzzle—and no answers. Moreover, the puzzle was smaller than the one in daily use, and unsymmetrical. Not intended for publication, then—and therefore for special consumption. She ran her eye indifferently down the clues. They seemed at first glance outlandishly cryptic. Not all of them solved themselves on sight.

> *Go for port with Spanish exuberance. (5)*
> *River doctor, backward one, in another river. Gone. (7)*
> *'There are in nature certain fountains of _____'*
>   *(Bacon) (7)*
> *Sub-slumber river, it. (2)*
> *Wind tubes round mangled feet for source of refreshment—and to look for vital clue. (9)*

There were others.

Well, *Sub-slumber river, it* was *Po; it* being a convention for *Italian*, so overworked that she had told all setters that she would not accept it again. It wasn't funny. It was just infantile. They didn't deal in two-letter words — and this one was totally isolated, not checking with any down-light. What did he think he was about? Did he really think she had time to waste on this sort of drivel?

River doctor, backward one, in another river. Gone.
(7)

That was simplicity. River was R. River doctor — RDR. *Backward — reverse: RDR — add one — IRDR.* So the other river had to be Dee. DEIRDRE. Gone, had she? So what did he think she was going to do about that? Rush madly to take her place, having worked out from this rigmarole where he was? Oh no, Mr Whippletree. Thank you for the Jumbo. That's saved a lot of trouble, but you weep alone for Deirdre.

She threw both his crosswords on to the table behind her. She was not going to look at either of them again in office time. She rang down to the Study Group to get someone on picture research. Pierrots. A whelk stall. Kids shrimping.

There was an hour to an hour and a half every morning when Forrester's office was free of Bransby-Lowndes. The liaison officer was off doing the other half of his liaising. Kenworthy took advantage, only to find Forrester entangled in other chores that were not going well. Special inquiries from Cabinet Ministers had a habit of coming in in bunches — and of requiring an answer the day before yesterday. How had that damned old Battle-axe in the *Any Questions* team got hold of the conclusions of the Webbe-Fulton Commission even before the report went to the printer? Was there any scrupulously legitimate way of seeing that a certain retired RN Captain did *not* repeat *not* appear on Sir Robin's late-night discussion panel? And a cheesecake walkabout was contemplated in the covered Market Hall in Halifax. Could an action list be supplied for dealing in advance with any smells, please?

'See how it is, Simon? One badly-fitting dustbin lid in Halifax, and I'm back to trying shopdoor handles. There's more and more coming in here that never used to be asked for. These things just used to get done—by someone else.'

'Paying the penalty for your own brilliance,' Kenworthy said. 'Have we got a date for the re-opened Parkeston inquest yet?'

'They're waiting for some of that ban-the-bomb crowd to get back from the Continent. They think someone might have seen something.'

'Is that likely?'

'Shouldn't think so. Otherwise they wouldn't be waiting for them, would they?'

Cynicism was a habit of mind, even among honest operators.

'It's all going to end up with *nobody knows*,' Kenworthy said. 'But somebody does. The man who did it does. And we know how these things work. They aren't exactly hushed up; they're just sat tight on.'

'Counter-productive,' Forrester said. 'I've always said so. If I were advising the young man who bashed King's head in, I'd say come out in the open with it. Get yourself charged with manslaughter, and get yourself acquitted. Stand your trial and come out clear. It's bound to work out like that. And that would shut all mouths.'

'No name's been mentioned yet, has it? Not even whispered?'

'No. That Finsbury mob were too dense to know what was happening to them. All they saw was a thrashabout of helmets, arms and trousers.'

'How about that community lawyer? Hasn't he got on to anything?'

'He's got to play it carefully. He must know he's going to lose all ends up.'

Forrester paused to read and initial another sheet of typescript.

'You and I know, Simon, it's the wrong way to do it. We wouldn't swap the British police for any in the world, would we? And yet there are some who never learn that the way to save your name is in public.'

He answered on his intercom a query from one of his team.

'We need to know, don't we, Simon, you and I? I mean, if we're to do anything about it, we need to know.'

There was a light of hope in Forrester's eyes.

'I think we do,' Kenworthy said. 'How are you fixed? It's many a year since we did a job together.'

'Oh, I can leave this place for an hour or two. I'm not a bloody slave to it.'

That was in running for the untruth of the month—but Kenworthy forbore to say so. Forrester farmed out one or two more trifling jobs, checked the state of play of a few others, then informed his acting deputy that he was out till after lunch.

'What the heart don't see, Bransby-Lowndes don't grieve.'

He took great breaths of outside air as he and Kenworthy made their way out of Westminster.

Timothy Walwyn did not look like a solicitor. But the penalties for deception in that walk of life are such that he must surely be one. On a crowded pavement, one would not have known. He did not look more than about seventeen. His hair increased the size of his head at least threefold and reminded Kenworthy of a picture of a native of Papua that he had once seen in the *Children's*

Encyclopaedia when he was a boy. He had not yet grown
out of acne. He was wearing blue denim jeans and a tee-
shirt that had faded from an original brownish shade of
purple. His sandals were thonged between toes that an
æsthete would have concealed from the world. Would he
have lost all credibility among his clientele, if he had
cultivated an edge of dignity? He was in the middle of a
characteristic day when Kenworthy and Forrester
appeared in his office. He was interrupted by a crisis or
two while they were with him. He did not seem to need
any manuals on squatters' rights or entitlements to
supplementary benefits. He was a man who did not
simply care. He passionately felt for the despair of his
one-parent families, his riddleroofed tenants and the
domestic hells from which some of his callers saw no hope
of escape.

He was obviously uneasy at receiving two police
emissaries, especially from an apparently extra-
Metropolitan part of the machine. They told him—with
brevity—as much as they honestly could about who they
were and what their angle was. They knew it was not
enough to make him believe—and he did not believe.
They said they wanted to get down to the truth of the
Parkeston punch-up, and he said so did he. The question
was thinly under the surface, had he heard of Forrester's
assault on Willy King. He seemed not to have done.

'Is Albert King still not cooperating?' Kenworthy asked
him.

'I can't discuss my clients with you.'

'Have you set any ears to the ground in the Parkeston
area? For coppers' names, I mean?'

'They weren't Parkeston coppers. You must know that.
It was a central riot squad, drawn from more than one
authority.'

'How come—for a potty little football match like that?'

Walwyn looked at the two with the kind of uncertainty

that preceded a decision of principle. Throughout the interview, he had been guided by the determination to give nothing away, not to be tempted by implied offers to trade. As he knew so little, there was not much that he could give away—which made him cling all the more jealously to what he did.

'I do know that they were tipped off,' he said. 'I picked that up from gossip among the rank and file.'

'A regional riot squad was tipped off that there was to be a major battle at the Finsbury-Parkeston match?'

'That's why they were turned out.'

'So they must have believed it. And that would explain why the force was vastly excessive for the task in hand. What was the proportion? Have you been able to work that out?'

'I'd say roughly two hundred to fifty. They kept a reserve, but it was a small one: I'd say less than a third of the force. I can't resist the thought that when they had mobilized the squad, they were determined to exercise it.'

That was about all they were able to learn from Timothy Walwyn. He was a young man of goodwill. He was one who did not count the cost to himself of what he was doing. But he did not know how to present either himself or a case. He did not know how to make allies. He was emotionally entangled with resentment of the malpractices that he was fighting. He was doing an immense amount of temporary good to the community he had chosen to serve. But very little of that would reach far or last long. Kenworthy and Forrester thanked him and left. He was delightedly under the impression that he had wasted their time.

CHAPTER 17

Chief Inspector Bert Wallace would have been many men's obvious choice to head a joint regional riot force. It would surely need only a couple of well-publicized outings to teach any young thug in East Anglia—which included a dirty slice of the Home Counties—that it was better to spend his spare time off the streets. Obviously Wallace had been someone's choice: the squarest of pegs in the squarest of holes. One set thieves to catch thieves: and one hired a bully to bully bullies. And anything smacking of creative thought about the situation was wet. Being wet was like being a prig. The label alone secured the verdict.

They visited him in his office in his home force, beyond the green-fields northern border of the Metropolitan Police area. Wallace began to bully Kenworthy and Forrester before they could begin to bully him. They told him precisely who they were and made no effort to turn Forrester's official position into a pulling of rank. Wallace's confidence, never lacking, was boosted as he saw what a couple of Cuthberts he was dealing with.

He led off with well-practised bile against the imbecility of a society that wanted to shackle men by their wrists and ankles before sending them out to ensure the peace. He begged to know what hope there was for a community that turned its wrath on its protectors and saved its tears for those who had started the trouble in the first place.

'You were certainly well manned for the task in hand at Parkeston,' Kenworthy said, as if he were making a joke of it.

'Why not? We have the men. They need the experience. They get pissed off, only doing it in a gym.

Why should we only attack with inferior numbers? Why shouldn't we go in to win for a change? Besides—'

'Besides?'

'These weren't just football scruffs. There were those Commies.'

'Commies?'

'Unilateralists.'

'Would they have given trouble, do you think? I'll grant you I think they're misguided. Also possibly unhygienic, unproductive, and don't dress in the best of taste. But all they want to do, surely, is sing folksy "Blowing in the wind" songs.'

'They make me sick,' Wallace said.

'And I believe you were warned there was going to be trouble?'

But Wallace was too old a hand to fall for anything as obvious as that.

'Oh no you don't. You've both been at it long enough to know that no officer reveals the name of an informant. That's something my own Chief Constable would know better than ask of me.'

'Maybe he wouldn't need to.'

'What am I expected to read into that?'

'If your Chief Constable is worth a tenth of his salary, he'll know already. You don't know why you were tipped off that there was going to be a bloody revolution in Parkeston?'

'Because there's still some public spirit left in the land.'

'Because a certain organization, which I need not name, is only too happy to see men doing what you did at Parkeston: steadily and progressively bringing us police into disrepute. Who was it came to see you? Dykes? Bellamy? Bragg?'

But Wallace was not going to be trapped like that. He was not even going to concede a debating point.

'I know the men you're speaking of. I've not set eyes on

a single one of them for years. But I'll tell you this, Kenworthy—I don't sneeze at what they are trying to do.'

Wallace became an exponent of sweet reason.

'I mean, look at it this way. In ancient times it was every man's duty to take his share in keeping the peace in his parish. Some men found it a bind, so they paid others to do their spell for them—hence the birth of the parish constable. What's happening now is a logical extension of that process. If the public doesn't like the way the police set about things, they start employing private forces in whom they do have confidence.'

'Which is why there are now more than seven hundred firms offering private security services in this country. A quarter of a million men in uniform are guarding money and the transport of money—in upwards of ten thousand armoured vehicles. Others are offering security clearance of personnel. They're the ones that frighten me most. And in face of this, the police must show that their own house is in order.'

Wallace's chest seemed to swell over his blotter. 'Are you suggesting that my house is not in order?'

'No whitewash? No cover-up? Have you brought forward the man who killed Geoffrey King?'

'An accident.'

'Are you setting yourself up as coroner, too?'

Wallace put his hands palms upwards on his desk, as if he were pleading on behalf of his own innocence.

'What am I to do with that young man? I don't know what happened: I wasn't there. I've talked to him. I've told him bluntly: the decision's his. He knows the score. He dropped the boy's head to run to the help of a comrade who'd been kicked in the goolies.'

'It must have enraged him, to see that happen.'

'Doesn't it enrage you?'

'I'll grant that I might have chucked the lad's head down a bit roughly myself.'

'And you'd have wanted to sacrifice your career for it? I tell you, Kenworthy, I'm sorry for that youngster. I can see us losing him. We can't afford wastage like that. As it is, he can't sleep, thinking he's killed someone, even accidentally.'

'So you do know who the man was?'

'Of course I know who it was.'

He was surprised at the change in Kenworthy's tone.

'And do you not have a duty to help a coroner's court?'

'I've a number of duties. A complicated web of duties. So have you.'

'I've one over-riding duty. And that's been a comfort to me more than once, when a decision came hard. The law of the land.'

'That's what we're all here for.'

A mixture of bluster and the harmlessly obvious: Wallace taking refuge behind the undeniable.

'So you'll be telling the coroner the whole truth,' Kenworthy said.

And that was the moment when Wallace first realized that these two who had called were truly *force majeure*.

'Because Forrester and I will be putting in statements that will get to the coroner.'

Wallace cannot have doubted that he was checkmated, but he said nothing at once. Kenworthy came back with a softer tongue.

'Why worry, Wallace? I don't see you need come off the worse. And you'll do your task force more good than harm. Provided you do the right thing.'

Police Constable Stephen Perry had been on loan to the task force from Hertfordshire, and one of the defensive measures taken after Parkeston had been to bring him back exclusively to his rural duties. Kenworthy and Forrester paid an evening visit to him at his village police house. Wallace had given them his name and address.

That had been part of doing the right thing.

It was a small home, contemporarily furnished, not to Kenworthy's taste, but brightly and airily, with picture-windows that by daylight must overlook a rolling flank of wheatfields. But there was an atmosphere in the house. Brightness and airiness were a memory of which the trappings were a hurtful reminder. Two children, a boy and a girl, ages probably about twelve and nine, were doing homework at the living-room table. They looked up from their books with a mixture of anxiety and hostility. They had grown accustomed to unsympathetic callers on their father. Their mother was a neat woman whom one pictured candidly sexy, ten years ago, but who had been sleeping unrestfully for the last few weeks. She was also probably one of those women with a simple fixed philosophy who are capable of little more than firm-jawed disapproval when it is being flouted. They can suffer great hurt when their disapproval is ineffective.

Perry took them into the small front room. There were police papers about. The lower glass shelves of an oak bureau held stacks of the sort of pro forma's that are used a lot in rural policing. Perry was a tired man who was obviously going to flare if many more obtuse types came to see him. He was the sort of man any commander would naturally be glad to have on his assault team. He was a scrum half who still played often enough not to have started running to fat.

'We know what happened. We hate making you run through it again. But we've got to. We need to hear it from you.'

'I'm not prepared to say anything except in the presence of my own Chief Inspector.'

'We've spent the afternoon with Mr Wallace. He'll be in touch with you. I'm surprised he hasn't already.'

Though actually Kenworthy was not surprised at all. Wallace would have gone round asking third and fourth opinions. There would be differences of judgement, some of which would have slowed the final decision down. But he'd be nudged back to Kenworthy's and Forrester's view in the end.

'So what am I supposed to do now?' Perry asked, with a touch of truculence — and also over-dramatizing his own helplessness.

'Tell us your story, and we'll answer that.'

He still did not know whether he ought to.

'I still don't think —'

'I think you'll find that Mr Wallace has had a complete change of heart since we talked to him.'

Perry looked into some incalculable distance.

'To tell you the truth, I'm probably going to pull out,' he said.

'There's no need to do that.'

'I didn't contract in for killing kids.'

He was a decent enough man, of no complex motivation. His code was mostly applied sporting rules. And he expected decent opponents to respect the referee, too.

'I did kill him. I've been wanting to openly say so since square one. I did tell the truth to Wallace. I told him I wanted to make plain dealing of it. He said that if I wanted to be a bloody idiot, that was my affair. He made me feel like a proper bloody nana.'

'Start from when you were warned for this special duty.'

'It was short notice. Tea-time. No chance to get a decent meal first. We were told there was going to be a big upset: soccer vandals on one side, anarchists on the other. There'd be a lot of the public about too — passengers on the night boat, trains in from London. We'd got to do a quick job, before any civilians got hurt.'

That was what they had all believed — Wallace included.

'I saw red when this spidery King youth brought

something out of a trouser pocket and threw it into the back of my mate's neck. I thought at the time it was a glass marble. Some of the yobbos were throwing darts. There was a bit of milling about, and when King saw that I'd spotted him, he tried to side-step round the crush. I brought him down in a rugger tackle.'

'On the railway platform?'

'That's where it was all happening. I then got hold of him under the armpits, and one of my oppos, PC Reynolds, got hold of his feet. We started to carry him into the report centre — he was struggling like mad — it was like trying to hold an eel. When we got him inside, he got one foot free and kicked Constable Tabrett in the privates.'

There was something of rehearsed witness-box fluency in the way he was talking now.

'I could see that Tabrett was very badly injured indeed: they had him in dock long enough for it. So I ran to his assistance — which meant throwing King down.'

Pause. The crunch. Literally.

'How hard?' Kenworthy asked.

'Pretty bloody hard. I heard the bone go. I can still hear it.'

Once or twice he had had to try hard to keep the crack out of his voice. But he said those last words firmly.

'I wanted to tell it as it was. I wanted to clear it. It could have happened to anybody. All I want to do is stop thinking about it. I shall have to jack it in, you know. The Force, I mean.'

This time, Kenworthy said nothing on that score.

'You will have to tell the truth,' he said.

'It'll be a relief.'

'There were signposts of the Perrys' life about the room: a wedding photograph posed under a lych-gate; a pair of cheap prints of white-walled Spanish villages; two finalist's amateur league medals. But most of what Steve Perry had ever done was sick on his mind.

'So what happens then?' he asked.

'One never knows for sure. The Federation will see you've a good lawyer. My guess is you'll get all-round clearance. There's something wrong with the system if you don't. Mind you, I wouldn't wax too poetic in the box, if I were you. No need to tell them you heard bone splinter. After all, you don't *know*, do you? What does matter is that you'll get clearance with yourself. And you'll have done the best you could for your Force. Whitewash never works.'

'I shall have to talk it over with Sue.'

'It'll be the best bit of news you've brought her for some time.'

Judith Pascoe was in bed early with her radio. She listened a lot to steam radio in bed. She was also playing with the first stage of her own next crossword. But her mind would not handle it. A certain amount of concentration was needed to deal with such configurations as -E-E-K-. And that kind of concentration was not hers tonight.

She had taken a brief look at Whippletree's odd missive, but only in passing, as she had brought it out of her briefcase. She had not given her mind to it. She refused to give her mind to it. Whippletree was not worth giving her mind to.

-L-R-SM.

It was hopeless. She got up to mix herself a low-calorie bitter lemon — and took Whippletree's crossword back to bed with her.

Italian river — PO —

What sort of childishness had got into him? DEIRDRE she had already extracted. And Deirdre was GONE. Big deal.

Go for port with Spanish exuberance.

Spanish exuberance simply had to be *olé* GO was GO. GOOLÉ. Ignore accents. Why Goole? Why the hell would anybody be having anything to do with Goole? Where exactly was Goole, anyway? She knew it was on or near the Humber, got out of bed again, looked it up in the atlas. Yes: there it was. Not many miles from Axholme—which was where Whippletree had posted the thing.

So while she was out of bed, she might as well look in the *Book of Quotations*.

There are in nature certain fountains of _____ *(Bacon)*

She did not in general favour quotations in crosswords. It seemed cheating to look them up, in Bartlett and Co, but if you chose out of-the-way things, your ordinary solver had not much chance.

Francis Bacon (1561-1626) _____ *justice.*

Now what was this?

Wind tubes round mangled feet for source of refreshment—and to look for vital clue. (9)

It could not be anything but an anagram. TUBES mixed up with FEET. She scribbled a random scatter.

$$T \qquad U \qquad\qquad S$$
$$E \qquad F \qquad R$$
$$B \qquad E \qquad\qquad T$$

Festubert: it danced up at her from the pattern. There was a vital clue at the Festubert. Not many marks to him for suggesting that: the drunk who'd nudged the table, the waiter bringing a fresh basket of rolls; somebody slipping something nasty into Percy's food or drink—

The rest of Whippletree's clues did not give her much difficulty. He had been, she had to admit, quite clever. The Down clues had no special meaning, but the Across clues, in order, spelled out a sort of telegram.

JUSTICE DEMANDS CHANCE PUT POINT OF VIEW. DEIRDRE

DESERTED. POWERFUL CONSIDERATIONS SUGGEST FESTUBERT. REPLY PO GOOLE.

Oh, sucks to Whippletree.

There was high-level conferring about the preservation of the Queen's Peace when the Parkeston coroner re-opened his inquest. It was considered bad policy for Wallace's task force to be brought out. In fact its continued existence was threatened in some local government circles, and the final decision had been postponed until after the verdict.

A phalanx of Finsbury scarves milled past the ticket-inspector on Liverpool Street station. It was standing-room only on the diesel shuttle from Manningtree to Harwich. It was a bad morning for the handful of passengers who daily journeyed on this line. These ruffians had only to see someone frightened, and the desire to frighten was doubled. Very few of them had much strength. There was no stamina here: hardly one of them could have sprinted a hundred yards or jogged a quarter of a mile without physical distress. What was it that they wanted? To show corporate superiority, in the belief that to be superior one had only to be different. It was sufficient to their purpose if they could only disgust the public at large. It was remarkable that they had cohesion as a group, for many of them hardly knew each other. It was the opposition to them that united them, the belief that they stood against the world. One scared old woman wanted to get out at the village of Mistley. They would not let her. When they saw her struggling to get her string bags together, they pushed her back into her seat and formed a cordon round her with knees and elbows. The train began to pick up speed out of her station and her fear could not have been greater if she were being deported for ever from her native heath.

When they reached Harwich, other groups were arriving by other routes, some by a cross-country train from the north. There were parties of adults as well as adolescents. One group bore the banner of some Penal Reform Society that no one had heard of. A knot of trade union demonstrators were holding high the magic word SOLIDARITY. And everywhere there were green and orange scarves—green and orange scarves from Doncaster, Tyneside and the North-West. KING GEOFF placards had been brought from all corners of the kingdom.

It was the jam-packed crowding of the streets that did more human damage than anything else. People could not move, and not all of them knew the way to go. The herd direction changed its mind more than once. The police drove a wedge that split the crowd in two, and the separated halves attacked each other. Shop windows were smashed as if by the simple act of passing them. Hands went in automatically past the jagged glass and helped themselves to what they could reach; more than one wrist was gashed. Police drew individuals from the edge of the mob and arrested them for possession of drugs, stolen property, any object that could with imagination be called a weapon.

The inquest itself did not take long. Three-quarters of the way through the morning, a uniformed superintendent came down the steps with a loud-hailer and announced that the coroner had ordered a police constable to be charged with manslaughter. He was already under arrest.

'You have got what you wanted. Now go quietly home.'

But if there were any who wanted to go home, they could not move against the counter-pressures. The damage done in Harwich, Parkeston and Dovercourt was mounting towards six figures. Three courts sat locally for two days, awarding fines and detention. An odd thing was that Natsecure had played only a walk-on part in the day's activities. Eight uniformed guards had hung about the Regency Wine Store. The rumour was current that they were armed with nerve-gas aerosols. But the threat was not proof against a broken window and pilfered stock. Otherwise, Natsecure was not in evidence. There was no sign of leadership of any of the incoming contingents. There was no coordination of the crowd.

The authorities at Chelmsford were already worried. Stephen Perry was committed to the Crown Court, and was to stand his trial in about three months' time.

'I've done what I said I'd do, and I've run out of time, men and imagination.'

Hewitson, of whom Kenworthy had heard nothing for two weeks, had finally asked him to drop by.

'We have re-enacted. We have played charades between the West End and Highgate. We have conducted every inquiry we can think of in the neighbourhood of Mather's home. We've put the staff at the Festubert through the hoop. We have even dug out other guests who dined there that night. We have even identified and talked to the drunk who knocked a crust of bread off Mather's table. And he was—just a drunk who knocked a crust of bread off Mather's table. There was nothing. Nothing.'

'Not to be wondered at,' Kenworthy said. 'London's a big and impersonal place. People see too many other people. And this already counts as a long time ago.'

'I know. But if you look hard enough, talk to enough people, send enough men independently of each other over the same ground, you can usually rely on a miser's pinch of luck. That's what we've been looking for, if the truth is told—a pinch of luck. And we've had none. Sorry, Simon. I'll keep the file open, of course, but I've got to go and do other things. Incidentally, the word's about that Cawthorne and friends are in trouble.'

'Creditors?'

'They're not getting the contracts they need. They've thought big, because it's no use thinking otherwise. They've spent money they've got to recoup. They have work in hand, but it's neither here nor there — not enough to pay their wages bill. They've put their shirt on getting standing Insurance assignments. All they're getting is odd jobs. The buzz is that the bankers have given them another quarter.'

'Does that give them time to cash in on Chelmsford? What about you and I going into private business, Hughie?'

'With our luck?'

Judith Pascoe knew before she even spoke to Whippletree at the Festubert that the date had paid off.

Oh, sucks to Whippletree, it had been. Yet within minutes of thinking that sociable thought she had been picking up her phone to ask by what service she could have a message waiting for a caller when Goole Post Office opened next morning. Not that she was aching to see Whippletree. Not that she would find it anything but a tongue-tying embarrassment having to sit through a meal with the wretch. She did not want to dine at the Festubert ever again, least of all with Whippletree. Her motives — if she had motives — were covered by a strong rationalization. She would have to tell Kenworthy that Whippletree had made contact. Kenworthy would be sure to insist on her doing what Whippletree asked. The police were always dead keen on reconstructions.

Then, the moment she arrived at the restaurant, she saw Whippletree standing at the bar, not more than a foot or so away from where Percy Mather had stood. And the date paid off at once.

'Why Goole, of all places?' she asked over her Noilly.

'Because *of all places* just about sums up Goole. Who'd look for anyone in Goole? I'm not sure that Goole really exists. It's like walking into a figment of a rather nasty imagination. Anyway, I wanted to see Axholme before dying. It's played a certain part in my life. And Goole was handy. Besides — I felt like doing penance. There was something poetic in being immured in Goole till you decreed my release.'

'You don't owe me any penance,' she said, as icily as she could. It was difficult to be icy with Whippletree over a dinner-table.

'Well — if you've forgotten, don't let me remind you.'

'You owe me nothing. Look — this is a civilized meal. Let's keep it on a civilized plane. That means certain obvious subjects are tabu.'

'Agreed. But let's do essential business. I brought you here for a purpose: to look for a vital clue. I thought you might remember something.'

'I know; I have; already. I've been a bit of an ass, actually.'

He avoided any temptation to be facetious; perhaps he was not tempted.

'I've thought only of the man who nudged our table. It was not until I saw you, when I came in, that I remembered someone else. Like you, Percy got here before me that night. And as I came in he was standing at the bar, with a sherry, talking to a man. I saw very little of him. He moved away as soon as I appeared. I remember expecting to be introduced, and it did not happen.'

'Some casual acquaintance of Percy's, perhaps.'

'I'm sure not. I had a distinct impression — and you know what I mean by a distinct impression — that they had been engaged in quite a keen conversation. And you know what Percy's capacity for keen conversation was. I doubt if he ever made a casual bar acquaintance in his life. No; this was someone Percy knew quite well."

'Some other diner? Did you see Percy catch anyone's
eye while you were eating? Did he nod to anybody when
you went out?'

'Not at all. We were alone among strangers. I'm quite
sure that the man at the bar had left the premises. And
I'm equally sure, now, that he had doctored Percy's
sherry.'

'Possible.'

'Well, somebody must have doctored something for
him at some stage, mustn't they? I'll bet you anything
you like, Master Whippletree, that he fixed Percy's
drink—and that he was the one who took a taxi to
Highgate to meet a friend in the Spaniards.'

'A man Percy knew?'

'I'm sure of it.'

'Not someone from the office? You can't have met
everyone yet—'

'If he were, he'd surely have had a word with me,
wouldn't he? He'd have asked to be introduced?'

'One would have thought so. But Judith—this isn't a
pub. Men don't come in here to drink at the bar.'

'I suppose a friend of the management might.'

'Yes. It keeps crossing my mind that someone
connected with the Festubert might be embedded in this
somewhere.'

A waiter came to recharge their glasses. They were
going Dutch, except that Whippletree had insisted on
buying the wine. Roussillon. Whippletree said that
limited regional *appelations* were too often overlooked.

'It could certainly have been someone the management
knew well. A policeman? I suppose detectives sometimes
drink at restaurant bars without dining. Or retired
detectives, who've known the management for years—'

'Now don't get carried away too fast—'

'But it's possible, Peter Paul.'

'I suppose it wouldn't be too complicated to put out a

feeler at the bar.'

'No. We mustn't do that,' she said. 'It would get back to the man concerned if we asked. Let's wait till we have the chance to tell Kenworthy.'

'Are you sure it wasn't one of the men you met at Egham?'

'I am quite sure it was someone I've never met.'

'Anyway—don't stop remembering. The evening's barely started—'

'What are you going to *do* with yourself?' she asked him presently. 'You have cut the Civil Service smartly from under your feet.'

'I still have my feet.'

'But where are they going to take you? Honestly, P.P.—who's going to employ you?'

He seemed to look older than when she had last seen him: even perhaps capable of taking himself seriously, of being more worried under the surface than he was pretending.

'You'll have to do something to keep the Deirdres of this world in the comfort to which they're accustomed,' she said wickedly.

'Ah, Deirdre. You must allow me to speak of Deirdre.'

'I don't see any particular reason why you should.'

'But I want to.'

'I'm sure. *Can't get Deirdre off my mind.* Good lyric, that.'

'It isn't like that at all. You know perfectly well it isn't. What I got out of Deirdre—'

'I think I know the answer to that. You don't have to mince matters with me, Peter Paul. I'm a big girl now.'

'Big enough to see things from a man's point of view? Not a very exalted one, perhaps?'

'I don't spend a lot of my time trying to identify with men's motives. I suppose it's a question of needing relief. We women don't have the same problem.'

'But you have others.'

'Admittedly.'

'So here we are on earth to help to solve each other's. Believe me, I have quite a few that Deirdre couldn't help with. Or Sandra. Or Janes One, Two and Three. Or a hazy memory of Sues.'

'You're in self-destructively honest mood.'

'Just offering myself for exploration.'

'Isn't it usually called clearing the deck?'

'Seriously, Judith — what do you ask of a partnership? I'd like to know your formula.'

'It isn't a formula. There has to be some element of magic. You can't mix that in a beaker.'

'Magic is where you find it. And magic apart?'

'I prefer to be mostly understood,' she said. 'And what isn't understood isn't to be interfered with. Privacy respected, in other words. Sensitive anticipation. It would be nice to have pleasant surprises on a fairly regular basis. Shared interests — enough, anyway, not to have to swan off alone for all my pleasures. And enough differences to have a chance of learning something new.'

'I can offer all that,' Whippletree said.

There was some talk afterwards about where they were going to spend the night. Whippletree was clearly not keen on taking her to his flat: she was too special, he said. He asked her if she was superstitious about their going to hers. She said no; and her neighbours were worse than she was. But weren't the villains still gunning for him? He said nobody knew he was back.

They were not going to go to the expense of a taxi. At their age, in their mood, the world was magic about them — more than Judith's element of it: even the thought of a walk through the squalor of the West End to the Underground. Archway Station on the Northern Line, and the bus — if one came — up the hill past Holy Joe's.

Then she suddenly changed her mind—before they had even left the Festubert. It was too much for Whippletree. He was fulminating inside.

'I must make a phone call.'

She went back through the restaurant doors and made two. Whippletree continued to think the worst of all women. The second call was for a taxi after all. She bundled him unceremoniously into it. And only then she explained.

'You don't use your eyes,' she said.

'Don't I?'

'There was a car parked forty yards downstream from the restaurant. With the bonnet up. That's the cheapest way of parking on a double yellow line—though you can't keep it up for ever. I caught the sight of the man leaning into the engine. It's the same one that Percy was talking to, that night at the bar.'

'I see. So what was the peculiar address you just gave the driver?'

'Kenworthy's house,'

'Good thinking,' he said.

Her message had been short and Kenworthy's understanding had been quick. He was waiting in his hall with his front door slightly open, listening for the sound of their car. He was listening in fact for two cars, but if the people in the second one were who he thought they were, they might call off their chase if they realized where they were being led.

But would they realize? The man in the second car had his faults. Some of them were going to carry him into the slammer before he was much older. His sins were relatively venial, but could get a man in difficulties in certain leadership situations. He was a man who did not care enough about the detail of other people's lives. He had probably never known where Kenworthy lived.

Kenworthy heard the taxi rounding the last corner. It

came cruising slowly alongside the kerb, looking for names on the gates. Another car was changing down for the same corner. A black Jag; it would have to be a Jag. Kenworthy switched on the light over his front door, came out along his garden path. The taxi was already at rest. Judith Pascoe was paying the driver. The Jag pulled out wide to overtake them, the window wound down. Kenworthy went to his gate and waved: not at Judith and Whippletree — at the man in the Jag. The big car accelerated, purred away down the road. They would start nothing here. They would have to make prudent assumptions. They would assume that Kenworthy summoned reserves in strength to his home.

'You know them?' Judith asked.

'Both of them. The man at the wheel is called Ashmore. He used to be a detective-sergeant: a man reputed to be fearless. In point of fact, he suffered from a common misconception: it could never happen to him. But it did happen to him. He took five hundred quid for a sneak-thief Nelson touch, and the sneak-thief ratted on him. He was invited to take his fearless talents elsewhere. The man who wound down the window and didn't wave back at me used to be a Commander. I used to be supposed to call him Sir.'

The kindness and hospitality of the Kenworthys knew no limits. It also added to the frustrations of the evening. But many people have to get up just once in the night, and Judith and Whippletree met on the landing. They were in a condition in which they did not like tearing themselves away from each other's company. After that, they had to be very, very quiet.

The next morning, Judith travelled to Millbank with the Kenworthyland commuters. What she had not expected was that Whippletree would be ringing for her

from the front desk within an hour of her arrival. She was
furious.

'If Burton finds out you're in the house, he'll have you
arrested. You ought to be on your way back to Goole.'

'Kenworthy says he's sure they'll lay off now. They'll be
scared rigid. And I want to go down and see them in II
(Science and Medicine). I've had a belated thought.'

'Well, watch it! If Burton's on the prowl—!'

'Oh, and another thing: Kenworthy says he's now
absolutely certain there's a hot-line from the Duchy to
Natsecure. It has to be located. Was it through the Duchy
switchboard that you booked us in at the Festubert?'

'It was.'

'Kenworthy thought so.'

Whippletree disappeared into the corridors of the
Duchy and was gone about half an hour. When he came
back, he was looking boyishly satisfied.

'I thought as much. It proves nothing—but it's highly
suggestive. Just one of those things one picks up in shop-
chat in corners. A month or two ago II (Science and
Medicine) did a chore for the Forestry Commission. You
know those tree-buffs are very conscious of their services
to the public—always laying out picnic areas, camping
sites, nature trails and what-have-you? Well, they're
bringing out a series of booklets about enjoying the
woodlands and one scheduled for next year is on edible
fungi. That's a very sensitive area; there are borderline
cases: one specimen is eaten in Czechoslovakia when
fresh, but under a standing ban in Western Germany,
just in case. So Forestry played safe. They had their
draft separately vetted by a number of government
labs—including our friends S and M.'

One would not have thought that Whippletree's life
was involved in any complexities. His delight was so
puerile that Judith laughed at him.

'One particularly nasty little growth on which they

thought they ought to offer a warning was *Boletus luridus*, which they describe as "edible with caution". The caution is needed, because if taken with only small quantities of alcohol it produces a delayed action nausea. It's especially dangerous for heart cases, as it affects the circulation. A few of the relevant juices in Percy's sherry that night—'

'But we don't know, do we, that any of it got into Percy's sherry?'

'We know that the ex-detective-sergeant who followed us last night was standing at the bar beside Percy's sherry. We know that the dangerous content of this *Boletus* was isolated in our own laboratory. We also know, don't we, that no documents handled by any of our sections would get back into the outside world without first having been passed upstairs.'

Another visitor to Judith's office before the morning was far advanced was Kenworthy—Kenworthy looking, and not only acting, as if he were enjoying himself. She had not actually been aware at any time that Kenworthy had been under strain: but he was out of it now.

'Covering fire. Reserves. Right hook. Left hook. Won't be long now. But it's going to be tricky. I wouldn't have Hewitson's job for a fortune. Not but what I didn't do enough lining up of papers for court in my time. By the way, there's a message from Elspeth. She'd got some cuttings for your window-box, but the time for putting them in isn't till next spring. I expect it's something you talked about.'

He looked with frank interest round the walls, shelves and corners of Judith's room.

'They've been given a reprieve in Chelmsford. The Perry trial is being brought forward and transferred to another circuit, to avoid any suggestion of local prejudice. Bedford. They'll be moaning like billy-oh there.'

Kenworthy had started his tour of the Duchy at the top, asking to speak to Sir Henry before he called on anyone else. This time the Permanent Secretary was genuinely immersed in a photogravure catalogue: candelabra by Dumé. But he put it aside the moment Kenworthy entered and brought his mind briskly to business.

'Glad to see you again, Kenworthy. I don't imagine you'd be here unless you were ready to tie things up.'

'It's certainly looking very hopeful this morning, sir. I've come to apologize in advance for some of the cats I'm going to throw among the ranks of your doves in the next hour or so.'

'You'll do what's got to be done, obviously.'

'I'm afraid I'm going to upset somebody.'

'It won't do any harm to inspire a touch of mettle in the place.'

'There'll be a sigh of relief going up in Chelmsford,' Kenworthy said.

'Oh? It strikes me as a hole-and-corner little place to stage riots in.'

'There aren't going to be any. The case is being taken away from the circuit.'

'Obvious move. Should have been thought of first time round.'

'Transferred to Derby,' Kenworthy said.

He went next to Burton. The Killer was neither feeding his pigeons nor frantically working. He was sitting in one of his armchairs, studying holiday brochures.

'You're still alive, then,' Kenworthy asked brightly. 'In my walk of life, I'm bound to suspect everybody. But there's nothing so suspicious about you as your continued existence.'

Burton laughed. 'I'll tell you one day how I managed it — if you don't find out for yourself.'

'I just wanted to warn you that I've Sir Henry's authority to wreak all sorts of havoc in your Duchy this morning.'

'Be our guest.'

'It should be all clear by the end of your working day. They'll be sleeping better nights in Chelmsford, too. Have you heard that they've moved the case to another court? Stafford. Is Thompson in his office, do you know?'

He stuck scrupulously to the proper precedence in the order in which he called on others in the Chancelry. Judith's turn was not until after Thompson's. And the last in the pecking order was Iliffe.

No one was under the impression that he had wrought any havoc.

Kenworthy did not go to Natsecure until after lunch. The outward aspect of their leased offices was of torrid activity — parade-ground stage-management to impress callers. Ground-floor clerks and guards had a leanly tough look. Key-chains shone efficiently against polished belts. There was evidence littered about that every appropriate aspect of their work was computerized. Kenworthy asked specifically to be shown up to Cawthorne, which was received uncertainly, though the message went up at once. There was a short delay, and Kenworthy was being taken up, handed from one guard to another at corridor-ends. It might not be so easy for him to leave this building, if they did not care for him to.

'Frank!'

'Simon!'

They shook hands heartily. In the old days, little more than boys — like that night before the war when they had patrolled the South Bank with their arms round the waists of policewomen — the enmity between them had been bitter. Later, as the stakes had pulled up and the jackpot had filled, they had cloaked things behind hypocritical bonhomie. Cawthorne had always been the winner, but Kenworthy had always been a shadow on his horizon that he could not get rid of. After last night, Cawthorne must know that the denouement—or, at least, an attempt at denouement—was near. But that only doubled the need for social ebullience.

'And what can I do for you, Simon?'

'A lot.'

It almost seemed too easy.

'You're not actually coming to me at the best of times.'

'I've been a bit of a donkey, you know, Frank. Always sticking out against that and the other—and ending up with a pension from which the poverty-line is distinctly visible. And you know—you must know—I've done the odd chore for this comic department of Forrester's?'

'I believe somebody did mention it.'

'Nothing permanent in it for me, of course. And I wouldn't want it. Bloody Crown servants!'

Cawthorne brought up the right kind of grim chuckle.

'So if there are any openings in your organization—'

That was not expected to take Cawthorne in for a moment. He must have been expecting this false request from Kenworthy for weeks. But he played the accepted counter-moves.

'If you'd asked me a year ago—even six months. I won't try to pull the wool over your eyes, you of all people, Simon. You'll have heard some of the scare stories, anyway. We are not doing well. I think we may have to fold: cut our losses and sell what we've made of it to one of the bigger operators. Mind you—there's no need to spread that round the City.'

'Of course not. But that was what I wanted to talk to you about. I can see a possible break-through for you—if you can get in in time.'

'What's that, then?'

Cawthorne had screwed up his eyes. He was going to

listen to this—very carefully. He could not believe that Kenworthy was really coming here with favours. Kenworthy's handling of any Trojan horse needed study.

'This ass Perry—his trial—it's hot off the wire they're not going to hold it at Chelmsford.'

'They'd be mad to.'

'Northampton. And you can assume that the Cobblers are going to be up in arms about it. If I were you, I should get Don Briggs and Dave Bellamy out there a bit smartish. There'll be big money for preferential defences. And for operational intelligence.'

'Well, thank you for the tip, Simon—'

He still did not look too happy about it.

'I'll get Don and Dave in in a minute, and you can watch their faces. But did you say Northampton?'

'That's right.'

'Are you sure?'

'I've seen the copy correspondence.'

'I've heard it said elsewhere that it's going to be Lewes. Trap any rioters between the town and the sea.'

'Northampton.'

The rest of the interview was largely a matter of flannelling his way through and out.

Lewes: that answered everything. Kenworthy had told a different tale in every office in the Duchy he had visited. Lewes had been the false pearl he had presented to Thompson. And that made sense. Ted Thompson the womanizer, the husband of West German pulp: he was the one whose wife kept him on not too taut a leash, but knew when a tug at the neck would not come amiss. There must have been times when Thompson—whose lifestyle could not afford a break-up of his marriage—had taken risks without being caught. Except by Cawthorne. Cawthorne was a master of blackmail. For years a lot of information had drifted Cawthorne's way. He knew who was worth watching. It had not been difficult for him to buy the services he needed from the Duchy of Axholme.

'Neat, Kenworthy,' Killer Burton said, his eyes laughing under their bushy eyebrows, his enormous nose nothing but genial. 'I'd like to have got there before you did, but I think I must be lacking guile. That file that fell into Mather's hands really was the works. There was much more to it than Whippletree told you. Percy didn't show him the whole thing. It was a policy paper got up for study by the management of Natsecure. It laid down the broad lines of how they were going to use civil commotion to their advantage. Do you know I even went and talked to Ted Thompson about it? He may look casual, but his nerves must be tempered steel. I knew we'd a mole here — and so few to chose from. That seemed to make it all the more difficult . . .'

There were loose ends to tie up. Hewitson arrested Cawthorne and ex-sergeant Ashmore. Some of the evidence was decidedly shaky. It was still not known how they would have killed Percy if he had not died on them. But there were many engines of death, some more subtle than others, in the stock-rooms at Natsecure. They included a little phial of juices, actually labelled *Boletus luridus*. Some men treasure too highly little things that have once been of service to them. They will not throw things away.

   PC Stephen Perry was acquitted by a firm-minded jury on a prosecution case that could have gone either way with him. He left the police force. When any sprawling organization is wound up, there are always some issues that remain unaccounted for. Among the former policemen employed by Natsecure, there were some who had built up the dozen or so squads of brawlers who had raised Cain at obscure football matches. Up to the present, these men have not been brought to the bar: and that includes one called Cartwright or Cartledge, who contacted Jimmy Maddock in his gym behind the Pakis' place.

Whippletree was reinstated, but it was considered inadvisable for him to continue to function in the Duchy. Kenworthy tried very hard to persuade Forrester to take him on as Senior Principal, in a special collator's job for which there was an established vacancy at the Faculty. Forrester agreed that Whippletree had certain imaginative gifts that could be useful. But the final decision has yet to be made. It rests with Bransby-Lowndes.

Sir Henry Woodcroft gave an informal sherry party for those who had been nearest to the action. He seemed to have relapsed towards his legendary persona, and talked mostly about neo-classical influences on Sheffield plate.

Judith was there, not wearing her glasses. She was waiting for contact lenses, Whippletree having said that he would prefer that.

Sir Henry asked her whether her father had been Pascoe of the 4th Queen's Own Hussars.

'No, sir,' she said. 'He was a lance-corporal in the Pay Corps.'